Memories

Sage Gardens Cozy Mystery Series

Cindy Bell

Copyright © 2016 Cindy Bell

All rights reserved.

ISBN-13: 978-1534794764

ISBN-10: 153479476X

Table of Contents

Chapter One

Samantha's eyes widened as a bright blue bird landed on a branch right beside the bench she sat on. With the warm breeze, the clear sky, and the music of nature surrounding her, it was shaping up to be a lovely day at the park. She smiled and turned her attention back to her book. As soon as she started to read the bird began to tweet. At first she enjoyed the sound. It was quite melodic. But after a few seconds it grew louder, and louder, until it sounded more like a shriek. The ear-piercing bird continued its harassment. When she turned to look at the bird she saw a pillow in front of her. It took her a few moments to realize that she was in her bed and the pillow next to her was far more real than the bluebird ever was. However, the shrieking sound remained, and was even louder. She sat up in bed, her mind still fuzzy with sleep. The approaching siren cut right through her daze. Her eyes widened as she wondered what might have happened.

Samantha grabbed her robe from the side of her bed and headed for the window to take a look. As she wrapped her robe around her she spotted Owen. The nurse ran at full speed towards the community center. Her heart lurched as she put together that the sirens and Owen's urgency meant someone from Sage Gardens was in trouble. Without a second thought she hurried out the door towards the community center. When Samantha pulled the door to the center open she almost ran into another resident, Reynold. She didn't know him very well, but the sight of him caused her to panic. His skin was pale and he looked dazed.

"Reynold, are you okay? Where's Owen?"

Reynold raised a hand and pointed towards the fireplace. She spotted Owen beside the fireplace hunched down towards the floor. She couldn't see whatever he leaned over because the couch blocked her view. She stepped closer, almost too scared to ask what was wrong. As she peered past the couch she saw another resident of Sage Gardens, May, sprawled out on the floor. She looked away, but it was too late to avoid the sight of a fire poker in May's chest. With a gulp, Samantha grabbed the side of the couch to steady herself.

"Is she alive, Owen?"

"No, Samantha." He sighed as he stared down at her. "It's too late."

"We were supposed to meet for coffee," Reynold rambled as he walked towards them. "I was supposed to meet her outside and then go for a coffee. But I saw the door open. When I walked in, I saw her on the floor. I tried to help her. I did." He shivered. "I tried to help her. We were supposed to have coffee." He stared blankly at Samantha.

"Samantha, can you just keep him calm for a few minutes, I need to try to keep the scene clear?" Owen asked.

"Reynold, come sit down over here."

Samantha touched his shoulder. When she did she felt how intensely he shuddered beneath his shirt. The collar of his shirt was soaked with sweat. "Let me get you some water."

Once Reynold was settled Samantha walked over to the water cooler and drew him a full cup. When she turned back he was still in the exact same position she'd left him in.

He mumbled under his breath as she pressed the cup of water into his hand.

"Just try to take a deep breath. I know it's hard, it's a big shock, but it's important that you breathe."

"She's dead, isn't she? How can she be dead? I was supposed to meet her for coffee."

"I know, I know, Reynold. Just breathe with me." As she tried to focus on him, the door to the community center swung open. Samantha stood up and walked towards the door to block the entrance from any curious onlookers. Many people were familiar to her, but her mind was too

4

in shock to place names to faces.

"It's best if we keep the space clear for medics and police please." After she ushered them out she turned back towards Reynold. However, something in the fireplace caught her eye. The flames were low, as if someone had just started the fire, but they were hot enough to burn a long coil of paper. Her first thought was that whoever killed May tossed that paper in the fire. It might be the only evidence available. She hurried towards the fireplace and without considering what might happen to her hand, reached right into the flames to grab the piece of paper.

***

As the sirens blared through the retirement village the noise threatened to wake many of its residents, including Walt, eleven minutes before his alarm was set to ring. He despised being off schedule, but once he was awake there was no chance of going back to sleep. However, this meant his entire day would be eleven minutes off. The thought bothered him. He got to his feet and peered outside. When he saw his friend, Eddy, walk past the window, he dressed quickly and tried to catch up with him outside. As he passed a group of residents he heard some chatter.

"Someone is dead in the community center."

"Maybe it was natural causes."

"That's not what I heard."

"What's going on?" Walt caught up to Eddy, who continued to head straight towards the community center.

"I'm not sure yet, but it's something bad. That's a fire engine, an ambulance, and a few police cars headed this way. It's no false alarm."

"It doesn't look good."

"I thought I saw Samantha go inside." Eddy looked back towards the community center.

"We'd better check it out."

"Have you seen Jo?"

"No." Walt frowned. "I haven't seen her for a few days, actually. Do you think she might be involved?"

"I hope not. Let's get in there before the police kick us out." Eddy opened the door to the community center, just as a few other residents tried to walk through it. He ducked out of the way to allow them past. Walt stepped in first and gasped at the sight of May on the floor.

"We were supposed to meet for coffee." The man seated a few feet away stared at Walt. Walt recognized him as Reynold, a resident who had recently moved in.

"Samantha!" Eddy's voice carried through the open space of the community room. "Get your hands out of that fire!"

Walt spun around in time to see Eddy grab Samantha's elbow and pull her back from the fire.

"Stop it, Eddy!" She shook free of his grasp and stomped on something on the floor. Walt walked towards them as tiny pieces of ash fluttered in multiple directions.

"What is that? A newspaper article?" Walt

crouched down to look at it. Most of it was burned beyond recognition, but the top of the paper was still readable. Samantha pulled out her phone and snapped a picture of what remained.

"Everyone clear the room please, everyone clear the room!" Paramedics, followed by several police officers burst into the community center. Eddy walked up to one of them.

"That newspaper was in the fireplace. It's almost gone. I think it might pertain to the case."

"Thanks Eddy." The officer nodded respectfully to him. "If you hear anything about the case just let us know. But right now, we need everyone out."

"I understand." Eddy nodded in return and herded Walt and Samantha towards the door.

Samantha looked over at Reynold who still sat in the same chair. His skin had gone from pale to gray. It looked as if he'd aged twenty years while he was sitting there. Her stomach twisted with anxiety at the thought of what might have happened that morning while she was still sound asleep, enjoying the company of a bluebird.

Chapter Two

Eddy, Samantha and Walt stepped outside and into a crowd of onlookers who formed a semicircle around the community center. Owen stood a few feet away deep in conversation with a paramedic. When the paramedic walked away Owen's shoulders slumped.

"I'm going to go talk to him." Samantha broke away from Walt and Eddy as they threw theories back and forth about what might have happened and who might have been involved.

"A robbery?" Walt frowned.

"Not likely. If they wanted to rob May, why wait until she was in the community center?"

"Then it must be murder."

"It's hard to dispute that with the weapon of choice and the way it was positioned. There's no way she could have impaled herself that way," Eddy said.

"What about Reynold? He might be the only witness."

"Not a very good one. With the shock he's in I'd be surprised if he remembered his own name. He must have shown up not long after the murderer took off though."

Walt's shoulders raised up close to his ears as he shivered. "And they may very well still be here, watching."

"You may be right." Eddy surveyed the crowd that gathered close. Did the murderer want to observe the chaos that he or she had created?

Samantha walked up to Owen as he walked away from the paramedic.

"Owen, are you okay?"

Owen was a young man, in his twenties, who was studying to be a doctor. He worked as an on-site nurse for the residents who needed a little extra daily assistance.

"Maybe if I got there a bit sooner, I could have saved her." His tone reflected exactly who he was.

11

His only desire was to help, and in this case he hadn't been able to do that.

"I'm sure you did everything you could, Owen." She patted his shoulder.

"Poor May. I just saw her yesterday."

"Oh yes, I suggested that she see you," Samantha said. "She said that she'd been having some heart palpitations and was concerned. Was she sick?"

"No, I don't think so. From what I could tell it was anxiety. I tried to get her to talk to me about what might be bothering her, but she ignored me and said she had to leave. Maybe if I had insisted, or sent her to her doctor, or something, anything, I could have prevented this." He turned his head away and drew a ragged breath.

"I don't think so, Owen," Eddy walked up to them. "There's nothing you could have done."

"Yes," Walt agreed. "No one is to blame but the killer, Owen."

"You did everything you could, Owen,"

Samantha said.

"Thanks Samantha." He looked up at the sky and took a deep breath. "I should go. I know the office staff will be arriving soon. You three, be careful, okay? No wandering around alone until we figure out what happened here."

"Absolutely." Samantha nodded. Owen headed for the office.

"Speaking of alone." Eddy tilted his head towards the villas just as Jo began to cross the street.

"Jo!" Samantha waved to her to get her attention.

"What's all the commotion?" Jo looked between her three friends as she paused in front of them.

Samantha reached out and took her hand. "I'm afraid May has been killed."

"May? Are you sure?" Jo's face grew pale.

"Yes, I'm sure," Samantha said. "I saw her

13

myself."

"How terrible." Jo clutched her elbows and looked towards the community center. "How?"

"With a fire poker." Samantha sighed. "Through her chest."

"Sam, the police are going to want to question you since you were there before they arrived. I'll stay with you, all right?" Eddy rubbed her shoulder. "This will all be over soon."

"I'm going to head back to my villa. Let me know if you guys find out anything new." Jo waved to them then started to walk away.

"I'll walk with you." Walt fell into step beside her.

"Thanks Walt." She smiled at him. When he locked eyes with her, he didn't smile back. Jo stared at him for a moment, then glanced away. Samantha noticed, but her attention was drawn to the officer that summoned her over. Eddy remained right beside her as they walked up. After she supplied her name, the officer looked between her and Eddy.

"You were both here when Owen found the victim?"

"No." Samantha shook her head. "Eddy wasn't with me. I arrived shortly after Owen, and Reynold was here of course."

"Can you please give me a thorough description of what you saw when you walked through the door?"

"Sure." Samantha relayed the scene she had walked in on. She left out the part about snapping a photograph of the newspaper article, but detailed noticing it and pulling it out. "I thought it was unusual as there isn't usually a fire in the fireplace unless there is an event going on and it is very cold, which is very rare around here. In fact, I don't think I've ever seen the fire lit before. I can only guess that someone quickly lit it for the purpose of burning that piece of paper. Maybe they even lit the paper and then threw it into the fireplace which started a small fire."

"It's a good thing you pulled that scrap of paper out, we've bagged it as evidence. If you hadn't seen it, it would have been ash by the time we arrived."

"I just wanted to help. May was a friend of mine, we were in the same book club. I don't know how someone could have done something like this to her." She gazed down at her slippers. "I can't believe she's gone."

"You say you can't think of anyone that would hurt her. Are you sure about that? Had you noticed anyone unusual around her? Maybe a stranger that took an interest or someone that had an argument with her?"

"No, not at all. Around here it's easy to spot a stranger. Everyone knows everyone. I hadn't seen any unfamiliar faces lately. In fact, if anything, things have seemed rather calm."

"What about any love interests? Were Reynold and her dating?"

"May and Reynold? No, I don't think so.

They'd been spending a lot of time together, but I think they were just friends."

"Are you sure about that?" He made a note on his notepad.

"I did notice that they got to be close friends pretty fast. In fact, May didn't come to book club a few times to meet up with Reynold. But she always told me they were just friends."

"Thank you. If you think of anything that might help, please feel free to contact me." He held out a card to her. Samantha took it and tucked it into her pocket. As the officer walked away Eddy steered her back towards the villas.

"Are you doing okay?"

"I just can't figure out why this would happen to her." Samantha frowned.

"Let's go back to your villa. We'll try to sort it all out."

"Yes, okay. Did you notice how short Walt was with Jo?"

"Walt? No I didn't. He's not usually like that with Jo."

"I know. It was strange."

"Don't let it bother you. I'm sure whatever it is they will work it out."

Samantha nodded, but her concern about it just joined the swirl of other worrying thoughts that occupied her mind.

Chapter Three

Jo noticed how each of Walt's steps were evenly paced, not too wide, not too short. Did he think about it? Did he time it? Or was he naturally so evenly paced?

"So, what's going on, Walt? I know you've got something on your mind." She looked towards a group of people that headed in the direction of the community center.

"I've been trying to reach you."

"My phone is having some problems."

"That's not true."

"How do you know?" She glanced over at him.

"I know. So why are you not being honest with me?" He frowned. "I thought we were friends."

"We are friends." She paused and turned to look at him. "Don't ever think that we're not, Walt."

"Where have you been?" Walt stared at her

even as she glanced away.

"I'm sorry?"

"You haven't been around for the past few days." Walt stepped in front of her before she could walk past him.

"Now you're acting like Eddy." She laughed and lifted her shoulders in a mild shrug. "I needed some time to myself."

"Now you're lying again." Walt folded his arms over his chest very carefully so as not to wrinkle his shirt. "Do you really think that I can't tell when you're lying to me?"

"I really think that you can tell when I would prefer it if you would mind your own business." Jo raised a thin, black eyebrow and stared back at him with just as much authority.

"I think that you should be able to trust your friends enough to let us know what is going on with you, Jo. You don't disappear like this unless you have a reason. No calls, no texts, nothing. Do you know how worried I was?"

"Yes, friends should be able to trust each other, and you should be able to trust me enough, your friend, that if I have a reason to disappear, I don't need to be questioned about it."

"What are you two fighting about?" Samantha walked up to them with wide eyes. "I could hear you all the way down the street."

"You could?" Walt's cheeks reddened. "I didn't realize I had raised my voice." He shot a look at Jo. "Now, you've gotten me upset. Do you know what an elevated heartrate can do to a man my age? Not to mention what stress does to the internal organs."

"Walt, relax." Jo rolled her eyes. "Samantha, we weren't fighting. Walt just feels I need to run my every activity by him."

"Can you blame me with a killer on the loose?" Walt shook his head.

"Well, where have you been, Jo?" Samantha looked into her eyes.

"Are you serious?" Jo asked.

"It seems like a fair question," Eddy said.

"You too?" Jo's eyes widened. "Why do you care?"

"Of course we care, Jo. You're my friend. And I'm curious by nature. You, my friend, are hiding something." Samantha smiled.

"So, what if I am? Am I not allowed to have any secrets?"

"You're allowed, but you're not likely to keep them secret with friends like us." Samantha jostled her shoulder. "Why bother trying?"

"She's right." Eddy looked over at her. "So, why don't you just get it over with and tell all of us?"

Jo sighed and looked between each face that stared at her. "All right, fine. But you need to understand that sometimes I need a little extra cash, and I certainly never expected anything like this to happen. Eddy, I would appreciate it if you kept this to yourself. I know you will have the urge to tell the officers investigating the case about it, but if you truly are my friend you will consider my past and not put me on their radar, okay?"

"I can't make any promises until you tell me what it is that we're talking about. I'm sure you can understand that."

Samantha rubbed Jo's shoulder. "We're your friends, Jo we're not going to do anything to put you in danger or get you in trouble."

"Ha." Jo lifted an eyebrow. "May spoke to me about a concern she had. I don't know why she came to me, but she said she felt she could trust me. She said that some of her mail and money had gone missing over the last few months and she suspected that someone was trying to access her financial information behind her back. She thought that I might be able to find out more than she could. So I agreed to look into it for her, in exchange for a small fee."

"So, you know something that might be important to the case?" Eddy interrupted in a brash tone. "That's important to tell the police."

"Eddy, if I thought I knew something that could help find the killer I would agree with you, but I don't. I had barely even started. Every lead I followed up led to a dead end. Some private eye, huh? I was going to talk to her today and ask her for more information about what she wanted me to find."

"Jo, you need to tell this to the police," Eddy said.

"But I have nothing to say to them. It will only make my life more difficult if I get questioned by the police. Can you understand that, Eddy?"

"Yes, I can." Eddy took a deep breath. "There's no reason to bring you into it if you have nothing to add to the case. I'll tell the detective that I've heard some rumors about some concerns that May had. That way you can be left out of it, but the lead can be followed up on."

"Thanks Eddy." Jo smiled. Being a retired cat burglar she never thought that she would appreciate that Eddy was a retired detective, but at that moment she did.

"Let's just do our best to get to the bottom of this. May obviously needed help and suspected there was a problem in her life. And it looks like she might have been right and that problem caught up with her," Eddy said.

"But what if we tread into information that puts us at risk, too?" Walt shook his head. "This entire case feels like one big secret that once unraveled is going to lead to terrible things."

"It already has, Walt. Don't you think?" Jo stared back towards the community center. "A woman is dead."

"I need to go lay down." Walt pressed his fingertips against his wrist. "My pulse is racing. I need to rest for a bit."

"I'll walk you." Jo offered him her arm.

"Thank you." Walt grasped the crook of her elbow. As the two walked away Eddy looked over at Samantha.

"Odd pair, hm?"

25

"Sweet." Samantha smiled to herself and watched as they disappeared down the path that led to Walt's villa.

"Let's get you home." Eddy began to walk towards Samantha's villa again. Samantha's mind churned over the past few days. She hadn't shared what she knew with everyone just yet, because she needed to figure it out for herself. Once they were in her villa, Eddy grabbed a few muffins from a cabinet and set them on plates.

"I know you haven't had breakfast, neither have I." He poured them both some juice and sat down across from her. Samantha watched how he moved with ease through her villa. She appreciated that she had a friend that was close enough to simply take over when he needed to.

"Thanks Eddy. I'm still having a hard time wrapping my head around this."

"Is there anything that you know about May that might have put her in a position that might have led to her being attacked?" Eddy pushed the plate across the table towards her. "You have to eat, Sam."

She broke off a portion from the top of the muffin and popped it into her mouth. As she chewed it she thought about the question that Eddy had asked her. "She did approach me about something. Now that I think about it, it might relate to that article that I found in the fire. She wanted to know how to find an old article. I suggested the microfilm at the library. I thought she was just doing some historical research, or maybe some genealogy since they just had that seminar about it."

"So, she might have been the one to bring the article into the community room. And to throw it in the fire?"

"I'm not so sure. Why would she go to all the trouble to print it if she just intended to burn it? It seems to me that she more likely brought it with her as proof of something, or to show someone else." She pulled her phone out of the pocket of her robe and scrolled to the picture she'd taken of

27

the remains of the article. It was hard to make anything out on it. "I've got the date, and the name of the newspaper. There's enough of the title to compare it to the articles in the newspaper to tell which article it was, too."

"Do you think she brought it there to show Reynold?"

"I suppose. That was who she expected to meet. But someone else showed up before he could get there. Maybe she burned the paper to hide the information."

"Or the killer burned it to stop her from revealing whatever she found," Eddy suggested.

"I wish she had told me more about what she was up to. Maybe I could have helped her with it."

"We all have thoughts about what we could have done to prevent such a tragedy, but that won't do anything to help. All we can do now, is figure out the why and the how. I'm sure that there's a reason behind everything."

"I'm ready to find out what that reason is,"

Samantha said.

"I think we all are. But first you have to eat." He pushed the plate towards her again. "I'll give Walt and Jo a call to see if they want to meet later to discuss it."

"Thanks Eddy." She took another bite of her muffin.

Chapter Four

When Walt arrived at Samantha's villa, he noticed the bushes in front needed a good trim. As soon as she opened the door he pursed his lips.

"Samantha, haven't you had the gardener out here lately?"

"That's not really my main concern today, Walt." She gestured for him to step inside. Jo perched on the edge of the counter beside the toaster in the kitchen. She eyed Walt the moment he walked in. Walt nodded to her, then turned his attention to Eddy at the kitchen table.

"So, where do we begin?"

"The only solid lead we have so far is this." Samantha held out a tablet that had a magnified version of the picture she had snapped. "I pulled this out of the fire and took this picture so that we could look into it. Recently, May asked me about looking up old articles, so my best guess is that she found what she was looking for and printed it out."

Walt scrutinized the image and then cleared his throat. "Not much to go on here, but it should be enough to find the article."

"I'm planning to go to the library when we're done here to see if I can track down the article. But before I do that, it might be a good idea if we all considered the past few times we've interacted with May, and whether or not there was anything that might have been overlooked at the time, but now may be a bit suspicious," Samantha said.

"I told you about my conversation with her." Jo pulled one foot up onto the counter.

"Jo, shoes don't belong on kitchen counters." Walt steadied himself on the back of Eddy's chair. Jo raised an eyebrow and smiled at Walt. She pulled her other foot up onto the counter as well.

"I wish I could still bend like that." Samantha sighed.

"Come to Pilates with me, we'll get you limber." Jo winked at her.

"Or, I could just sit in a chair and skip all of that sweat-inducing stuff." Samantha plopped down in the chair beside Eddy. "Ah, yes, this works just fine."

Jo laughed and gazed at Samantha fondly. She was the closest thing to a sister she'd ever experienced. Suddenly, her eyes widened. "Her brother visited her recently. It was only a few days ago. Remember?"

"Oh yes. What an oaf he is." Samantha's lip curled and she shook her head. "I know I shouldn't talk that way about him now that he's lost his sister, but he was so unkind to her."

"Unkind how?" Eddy leaned closer.

"We were having our book club coffee morning a few days ago when he arrived. The entire time he criticized her, told her that she was forgetful, that she was stupid. It was really uncomfortable to be around them. He kept making comments about how she forgets to pay her bills, or left the tap running when she went out to get the mail. Just embarrassing little things that shouldn't be aired in public."

"Well, some siblings are like that." Eddy shrugged. "That doesn't mean that there was anything more to it."

"I think in this case it might." Jo eased down from the counter and walked over to the table. "When she came to me she mentioned that she was worried about someone getting into her finances and so forth. She couldn't give me a good explanation as to why, or wouldn't. She seemed very confused and anxious. She mentioned that I should look into her brother as part of my inquiries. I think she suspected that her brother was up to no good."

"Forgetful, confused, anxious." Walt pulled the chair out that he leaned against and sat down. "Those could all be signs of old age taking its toll. We should consider that maybe her brother wasn't just being mean, but noticed a change in his sister's cognitive health."

"I hadn't noticed any real decline." Samantha glanced at Jo. "You?"

"No, not really."

"Sometimes it's hard to notice it when you see the person often. It can be a distant relative or friend that sees the decline more because they are not there for the gradual change. All I'm suggesting is that we consider it," Walt said.

"Okay." Eddy nodded. "Good observation, Walt."

"Even if he did notice a change in her, that still is not an excuse for the harsh way he treated her. There was some obvious bad blood between them. Samantha saw it, too, right Samantha?" Jo said.

"Yes, and I may have an idea of what was part of the problem. Before he left I overheard them arguing about some antique jewelry and land they own together. I think it had something to do with one of them wanting to sell and the other not wanting to. But to be honest I don't know which. I kept moving because I didn't want to have to talk to him again," Samantha said.

"So, the brother is more than a little troublesome." Eddy frowned. "Is he local? Could he still be in town?"

"Yes, he lives about twenty minutes away, but I'm not sure if he's currently in town or on vacation," Jo said. "It's obvious that May suspected her brother of ill intentions while she was still alive. It might be a good place for us to start to suspect him of her murder."

"It's the only place we really can start," Samantha said. "Otherwise, who else could it be?"

"I don't think that someone just wandered into May and decided to kill her, and it wasn't a robbery. It seems to me that someone might have had a score to settle. Don't you think, Eddy?" Walt glanced over at him.

"That would be my best guess. However, there's also Reynold."

"Her friend?" Jo tilted her head to the side. "Why do you think that?"

"I think it because he was there, at the scene of the crime," Eddy said. "First rule when investigating a homicide, look at the nearest person. It's not innocent until proven guilty, but a process of elimination. Until we can eliminate Reynold as a suspect, he should be on the list."

"Only because he tried to help May." Samantha tapped her fingers on the table. "When I saw him he was so shaken I thought perhaps he would pass out. I don't think he had anything to do with it."

"Maybe not, but we can't know for sure until we investigate," Eddy said. "Maybe I'm being paranoid, but there's something about him that just sits wrong with me."

"We should be delicate with him, though. He seemed very upset by the murder. We don't want to make things worse for him," Samantha said.

"I can be delicate." Eddy tightened his lips.

"I know you can, Eddy." Samantha smiled sweetly at him. "But I think talking to him about the murder would be better left to me."

"I don't think that's a good idea, Samantha. You already have too much sympathy for him. You witnessed his reaction and have a bias. I think it would be better for someone else to talk to him about it. Maybe Jo?" Eddy said.

"Sure." Jo shrugged. "Me and perhaps Walt? What do you say, Walt?" Jo looked over at him.

"Me? Why?" Walt's eyes widened.

"Because, you're very good at spotting a liar." She laughed. "Or, so you tell me."

"Fine, I'll do it." He looked into her eyes for a long moment, then broke into a smile.

"Okay, it's settled then," Eddy said. "I'll find out what I can from the detectives. Samantha will hunt down a copy of the article and May's brother's whereabouts, and you and Jo will question Reynold to see if he knows anything else about the murder."

"Sounds like a plan." Samantha stood up from her chair. "I'll head to the library now. Jo, do you know which is Reynold's villa?"

"Yes, I remember. Ready Walt?"

"Shouldn't we prepare a list of questions? I could look up the best ways to interrogate..."

"Let's go, Walt." She grabbed his hand and he instantly silenced. "I'm sure we can figure it out."

"Right, we can. Whatever you say." He smiled. As the two left Samantha and Eddy exchanged a look of disbelief.

"Stranger and stranger." Samantha shook her head.

"Remember, we have a murder to investigate, that trumps odd behavior."

"Okay, okay. Let me know what you find out at the police station."

"I will." He paused just outside the door. "I hope you didn't take what I said about you and Reynold personally."

"I didn't. You tend to have a clearer head in these situations, Eddy, and you're right. When I look at Reynold all I will remember is the fear in his eyes. I've already made my judgment about him so it would be hard to question him."

"I'm glad you understand that." Eddy tipped his hat to her. "I'll call in a little while."

Samantha nodded as she walked towards her car. Her mind already spun through the different ways she could hunt down information.

Chapter Five

The library was fairly empty when Samantha arrived. She noticed the librarian behind the desk, and smiled at her, then continued on to the microfilm reader. She pulled out her tablet and scrolled to the picture of the burnt article. She then searched the microfilm for the newspaper the article was written in. Then she checked the date. When she came to the right newspaper, she began the task of sorting through articles that were available. By the time she got to one that matched the few pieces of text that survived the fire, her eyes were a little sore from the search. However, one word in the full title of the article stood out to her the most. Death.

Mariner Man's Drowning Death Ruled Accidental

Samantha skimmed through the information

in the article. It recounted the story of Jacob, a young man who was out fishing and fell out of his boat and never resurfaced. It was reported that his brother, John, who was on the boat with him thought he was joking around and would emerge from the water at any moment. By the time he realized that was not the case it was too late. There was no mention of May in the article. There was no indication of why May would have been interested in the article. The dead man's name was Jacob Smith, a fairly common name.

Samantha printed the article, grabbed it from the printer, then settled down at one of the computers. She began to conduct a search on both May, and Jacob's history. However, it was much more difficult to follow Jacob's history. He was twenty-six when he died, and because it had been so long since his death and there was very limited information from that time available on the internet she couldn't find any history to dig up. This made it difficult to find a connection between him and May. The more she searched the more discouraged she became. As much as she was certain that there had to be some connection between the two people she found that it was nearly impossible to get any information and identify that connection.

When Samantha finally looked up from the computer she recognized that it had been over two hours. Her shoulders ached from being hunched towards the screen for so long and her eyes burned from staring at the monitor.

With no success in making the connection she refocused her attention on May's brother. She discovered the address of the property that Daniel and his sister owned. Its previous owners were their parents.

The fight between Daniel and May appeared to be over an inheritance. Samantha continued to search through Daniel's past to see if he had any criminal record. There was very limited information available, but she did manage to locate some court records that had been uploaded to the internet. Although he'd never been convicted of anything he did have some tangles with the legal system. The first tangle was in his late teens when he was accused of participating in fraud. From what information she could find she gathered that he was involved in some kind of pyramid scheme that went sideways. From what she could tell others involved in the scheme were arrested, but Daniel was never convicted. She saw no mention of May being involved, but there was still a chance that she was. As she looked over the information in the court records she recognized that the court proceedings took place in Mariner County. The name sounded familiar to her. She glanced down at the article she had printed out. *Mariner Man's Drowning Death Ruled Accidental.*

There it was. A tiny thread. It wasn't enough to explain why the article mattered to May, but it did throw Daniel into the mix. However, the dates were almost two years apart. The thread was thin and frayed at best. Still, it was there. There had to be more to it than that, but she wasn't going to find it in the library. She packed up her things and headed back to the parking lot. As she pulled open the door to her car she noticed a familiar face a few parking spaces over. Valerie Brunis. She was not exactly a friend, but she was in the same book club as May and her. May and Valerie had been quite good friends when Samantha joined their book club. Samantha tried to get into the car before Valerie spotted her.

"Samantha! Samantha!" She waved her hand through the air.

"Hi Valerie." Samantha turned to face her. "How are you?"

"Just shaken over this whole thing to be honest. And you?"

"A bit upset." Samantha nodded.

"I bet you are. I heard you were there this morning. How do you get into the middle of these things?"

Samantha rested her hand on top of the car. "I'm not sure. I guess I should figure that out."

"I have to be going." Valerie glanced at her phone, then smiled. "I have to meet someone."

"Have a good afternoon, Valerie."

"I will." She turned and walked away. Samantha did not overlook the fact that Valerie didn't wish her a good afternoon in return. Then again, Valerie wasn't the polite type. In fact, she'd been terribly rude to May the past few times they'd all been together. She didn't know what the problem was between Valerie and May, but Valerie seemed to be the instigator. She got into the car to drive back to the villa just as her cell phone rang.

"Hi Eddy, what did you find?"

"Not too much more than what we started with I'm afraid. Other than that the killer was likely about the same height as May. The medical examiner based it on the way the fire poker went in. So we're not looking for someone very short or very tall. It could be a man or a woman. Doesn't rule many people out does it?"

45

"What about information about her brother Daniel? I found that he was charged with fraud in his late teens."

"Yes, I found that, too. Apparently, he got several people including family members tied up in it, too. Poor kid was in over his head before he even knew it. It's seems that he's never been able to resurface from the fines and bad credit. He's in a vicious cycle."

"That might explain why he was so determined to sell the property. It's definitely in both his and May's names. I found the record for it," Samantha said.

"Yes, and that gives him motive, because with May gone it will be his now and he can sell it as he pleases."

"I also found a connection between the article I found and Daniel, but it is very thin. Daniel was charged in the same county that the article was written in. It looks like the article is about an accidental drowning death. I have no idea how it could be related and the two incidents are over two years apart."

"I wonder if there might have been more pages? Maybe what we have left isn't the only article that she wanted?"

"Maybe." Samantha looked out through the windshield at the traffic that passed by. It always surprised her how life carried on no matter what. "Why don't we meet for dinner? Everyone, I mean."

"Yes, we can do that. I wonder what Jo and Walt might have found out from Reynold. At the diner?"

"Yes. I'll head straight there and get us a table."

"See you soon."

Samantha started the car and pulled out of the parking lot of the library. She wondered if it was worth mentioning to her friends her run-in with Valerie and how May and her hadn't been getting along leading up to her murder. As unpleasant as Valerie was that didn't make her a murderer. Was it right to cast suspicion on someone she might even call a friend in the right circumstances?

Chapter Six

When Samantha pulled into the parking lot at the diner she noticed that there were quite a few cars. She wondered if she would be able to get a table for them after all. As she pushed through the door of the diner she was greeted by a loud cheer. A birthday party. Samantha waved to the hostess.

"I need a table for four, please."

"It's a little noisy in here right now. Do you want to sit in the private section?"

"Sure. That would be great."

The waitress nodded and led her into a separate room. "I'll bring the others in when they arrive."

Samantha sat down at one of the three tables that were in the room. As she gazed around the room she wondered why she'd never been in it before. It was a small space, but it was cozy and the walls were decorated with historical photographs of the town. She smiled at the sight of a group of young people lined up by an old fashioned bridge. She guessed they were in their late teens. The photograph reminded her of the age that Daniel was when he had his run-in with the law. Nineteen. That was very young to already be charged with fraud. What was his life like at that time? Who were his friends? Were they the ones that drew him into the pyramid scheme? Or was he the mastermind behind it all?

"Hey, nice place." Eddy made his way into the room. "Jo and Walt will be here in about five minutes."

"How did their talk with Reynold go?"

"I don't know. You know Jo, she only likes to text now, and I can't figure out what half of those abbreviations mean."

"I'll have to train you better." Samantha smiled.

"Give it your best shot." He chuckled as he sat down beside her. A few minutes later Walt and Jo arrived. Once the four were settled Samantha updated them with the information she had found, as did Eddy.

"So, how did your conversation with Reynold go?"

"Apparently, Walt is not the human lie detector he claimed to be." Jo smiled slightly.

"It was impossible to tell if he was lying." Walt sighed and hung his head. "I've never seen someone so unreadable before."

"What do you mean?" Eddy furrowed his brow.

"He was just so, vacant. That's the best way I can put it. I kept trying to discern his mannerisms, to predict when he was truthful and lying. He acted the same way when he said his name as he did when he said that he had nothing to do with May's death. The man is like a fortress, and I have to admit, I couldn't figure it out."

"What about you, Jo?" Samantha met her friend's eyes. "You're pretty good at telling a con."

51

"Yes, I am. To be honest, he left me unsettled. He was forthcoming, and shaken, but it was almost too perfect, as if he was trying to convince me of something."

"I'm sure the police have him on the defensive. Being a murder suspect can make you want to convince anyone and everyone you can that you are innocent." Eddy nodded to the waitress as she walked up. They placed their orders, then returned to the conversation.

"I still find it hard to believe that Reynold would do anything to hurt May. Not only that, but I didn't find any link between Reynold and May. Why would he kill her? However, I did find out that her brother Daniel was involved in scams, and desperate for money. He wanted her to sell the property and jewelry, she wouldn't, he killed her. It seems pretty simple to me." Samantha shrugged and drummed her fingers on the table.

"So, I don't think he would have done it that way. He could have easily planned it out." Walt pushed a napkin towards the center of the table.

"If you know your victim the way that Daniel knows his sister there is absolutely no reason to kill her in a public place. The risk involved would be immeasurable."

"That's if he thought about it first." Samantha shook her head. "Maybe May invited him to join her and Reynold for coffee. Maybe she thought that would break the tension between them. But Daniel arrived early, and they argued, and he decided to end things."

"Even knowing that Reynold was on his way?" Eddy frowned. "That must have been some fight."

"A fight, that possibly centered around this man." Samantha pushed the article into the middle of the table in place of Walt's napkin. "This is the article that was burning in the fireplace when I arrived at the community center. I have no idea how it relates to the case, other than that two years prior Daniel was accused of fraud in the same county."

"Hm, that is a big stretch." Jo gazed down at

the article.

When the food arrived the conversation dwindled. Samantha's mind flipped through ideas as she ate. If Daniel was the killer, why did he act so rashly? If he wasn't, who was? Could the suspicion around Reynold be valid? As disturbed as he was when she saw him, could it have been an act? Or was he disturbed because he had just committed murder?

"Statistically, family is more likely to perpetrate a violent murder," Walt said. Samantha blinked and looked across the table at Walt.

"What?"

"Oh, I was just saying that if you do the research on murders over the age of forty-five, it is more likely that family is involved. Mainly because at that point you are dealing with long term feuds, as well as inheritance battles."

"Then our main suspect has to be Daniel." Eddy looked around the table. "He has motive, opportunity, and although his actions may not make sense to us, they still need to be investigated."

"If we really think the brother had something to do with this, there's one good way to find out." Jo pushed her empty plate away. "I'll invite myself in to look through some things."

"Are you sure you want to do that?" Eddy raised an eyebrow. "You don't want to put yourself at risk, remember?"

"Oh, I don't mind. It keeps me sharp, for when I need to go back to robbing jewelry stores. I wouldn't want to get out of shape."

"Jo." Eddy shook his head. "I don't want to hear about that."

"That's why I say it." She winked at him. "If my career as a private eye doesn't work out, I'm going to have to come up with something."

"Very funny." Eddy smiled slightly.

"Maybe we should go tomorrow in the morning. From what I researched about him when I was looking into things for May, I discovered that he has a habit of going to the grocery store at the same time each week," Jo said.

"Good idea." Samantha nodded.

"Just remember that murdering your sister can really throw off your routine. He might not be following the same habits," Walt said.

"Maybe we should try luring him out of the house, so that we can make sure that he's not there when Jo breaks in?" Samantha snapped her fingers. "I could go to him, as a grieving friend, and ask him to share coffee with me."

"That might work." Jo smiled.

"You're going to have coffee alone with a potential murderer?" Eddy shook his head. "I'm not sure I like that idea."

"You think he's going to kill me with creamer?" Samantha grinned.

Eddy locked eyes with her. "I'm not joking. This man might have killed his own sister, I think that you need to realize that if he'd be willing to do that, he's capable of anything."

"I understand that." Samantha looked right back into his eyes. "I also understand that I'm capable of keeping myself safe." She smiled a little. "I also appreciate your concern, and that you want me to be safe. It means a lot to me, Eddy."

His expression softened as well. "I know you can take care of yourself, Samantha, but it still makes me nervous."

"I could go with her. I rather enjoyed the act when I spoke to Reynold," Walt said.

"Perfect." Samantha nodded. "See? I'll have back-up. Eddy, you can be Jo's back-up."

"I work alone, remember?" Jo raised her hand.

"Not anymore you don't." Eddy smiled at her. "You're stuck with me."

"Great." She rolled her eyes. "I can't wait."

"So, it's a plan then?" Samantha looked between them. "Tomorrow morning Walt and I will invite him out for coffee, and while we're gone, Jo and Eddy will search the house."

"I guess." Jo sighed and eyed Eddy. "But I'm in charge."

"Aren't you always?" Eddy finished his meal and stood up from the table. "Meanwhile, I'll check into this drowning, and see if I can find a connection to May or Daniel."

"Good plan." Walt nodded.

"If anything comes up before tomorrow morning, I'll let you know. I've got dinner." Eddy nodded to his friends as they dispersed. He handed the hostess some cash to pay for the meal. Eddy never ceased to surprise Samantha, he used to be very tight with his money. Maybe he didn't want Jo to have to pay for her own dinner, considering she was worried about money.

"Thanks for giving us this private space," Eddy said to the waitress.

"Honestly, we had it reserved for a grieving family, but they canceled at the last minute."

"A grieving family?" He looked into her eyes. "May's family?"

"Yes, I think that was her name."

"Did they say why they canceled?"

"It was for her brother and a few other people. He called and said that he'd changed his mind. That's all."

"How did he sound?"

She shifted from one foot to the other. "I'm not sure I should be saying all of this." Eddy reached into his wallet and set a twenty-dollar bill down on the table.

"It's just between us."

"He sort of laughed."

"Laughed?" Eddy raised an eyebrow.

"He said, I guess nobody cares that much, and kind of laughed, then hung up the phone." Her cheeks reddened. "I thought it was awful, but I figured people have different ways of grieving."

"Thanks for the information."

"Thanks for the twenty." She snatched it up from the table.

Eddy left the diner with his mind focused on Daniel. What kind of man laughed at his sister's death? A man that had killed her?

Chapter Seven

The following morning Samantha parked her car in front of Daniel's house.

"How do you drive in this thing?" Walt cringed.

"Sh! Walt, don't worry about that now. We're here." She glanced in the rearview mirror to be sure that Eddy and Jo were still close by. Once she was sure they were out of sight on the side street she opened her car door. Walt pulled a tissue out and opened his as well.

"I could have this car cleaned for you."

"Walt." She stared at him.

"What?" He met her eyes.

"Let me do the talking, okay?"

"Sure." He shrugged and followed after her. She knocked hard three times on the large, wooden door, then waited. A few moments later the door swung open. Daniel stood before them with his eyes narrowed and a faint sneer on his face. She assumed he did not like surprise visitors.

"Hi, Daniel?" She met his eyes.

"Yes? What is it?" He looked between the two of them with his brow furrowed.

"I'm sorry to bother you. My name is Samantha, and this is my friend, Walt. We are residents at Sage Gardens and we were friends of your sister, May. We just wondered if we could take you out for coffee."

"Coffee? Why?" He put his hands on his hips.

"Because we are upset about May, and we wanted to be able to offer you some comfort. May told me that your parents are gone, and you were her only sibling. I thought it might be difficult for you now that you're alone."

"We're all alone eventually." He shrugged and shoved his hands into his pockets.

"Still, it would give me some comfort if you'd share some memories of May with us. If it wouldn't be too difficult for you."

"Who is paying?" He eyed them with a stern expression.

"We will of course. It's our treat." Samantha patted her purse.

"Okay. I could use some coffee. But we can't take my car, I don't have much gas."

"That's okay we can go in mine," Samantha said.

"Okay." Daniel pulled the door closed behind him, then turned to lock the deadbolt. As they walked away from the door Samantha could have kicked herself for not trying to make the break-in easier for Jo and Eddy. Then again, knowing Jo, she already had a plan. Walt escorted the man to Samantha's car. He pulled out a tissue to open the door for him. Daniel gave him an odd look, but nodded as he got into the car. Walt sat in the backseat while Samantha got behind the wheel. She drove to a coffee shop that was a little further away to give Jo extra time if she needed it.

"So, you knew May well?" Daniel asked.

"Quite well, we were in the same book club." Samantha tightened her grip on the steering wheel. "I have a hard time believing that she's gone, and in such a horrible way."

"Yes. I told the officers I didn't want to know the details. Poor May."

Samantha glanced over at him. His words were sympathetic, but his tone was not. "You two weren't close?"

"When we were kids, sure. She was older then me so she used to look out for me. We used to spend a lot of time together and were always getting into things together. But once we became adults our interests went in different directions. I tried to keep a friendly relationship going between us, but it was rather difficult, since we had nothing in common."

"What a shame. She was wonderful to talk to."

"Maybe to you. But to me she was always so cold. She could hold a grudge that lasted for a very long time."

"Did you have a falling out?"

"Something like that. But it was so long ago, it's hard to believe she still harbored it."

"Too bad you two didn't get to settle things before she passed."

"I tried. That's why I went to visit her. I wanted everything to be settled. But she was so hardheaded, she wouldn't listen to a thing I had to say."

Samantha parked in a space in front of the coffee shop and looked in the rearview mirror at Walt. Walt nodded and climbed out of the car.

"I have a sister, too." Walt opened the door for Samantha. They walked around the front of the car to Daniel and Walt continued speaking. "She's rather difficult to deal with. Her life is a total mess, and I think she's just waiting for someone to fix it."

"Exactly." Daniel sighed. "She had fantasies of a man whisking her away and making her happy. Then she moved into Sage Gardens which I thought was absurd."

"Really? I enjoy it there." Samantha opened the door to the coffee shop and they filed in.

"It seems like a nice place, but not exactly affordable. I tried to tell her that she needed to save her money, but she never wanted to listen to me."

"How frustrating." Walt clucked his tongue. "There's nothing that bothers me more than fiscal irresponsibility."

"Exactly." Daniel sighed and sat down at the table. "But what can you do? She had her own mind and made her own choices."

Samantha ordered her coffee and did her best to bite her tongue. From her recent research she was fully aware that Daniel had not made the best financial decisions in his life, and yet he was trying to paint his sister as the irresponsible one. She reminded herself to keep an open mind and not predict what Daniel would say. To investigate she had to be willing to listen, and not assume.

"Did you two fight often?" Samantha asked trying to get him to open up.

"Just a spat here and there. Nothing I said to her would do any good, anyway. She still would have stumbled blindly into crisis after crisis. Not to mention the men she would date."

"Was she seeing anyone?" Samantha leaned forward some.

"Wouldn't you know better than me?" Daniel's expression shifted to one of suspicion. "I thought you said that you two were friends."

"Oh we were, but she was rather private about some things. I don't like to pry." She sipped her coffee to hide her face.

"I see." Daniel continued to stare at her. "Well, as far as I know she wasn't seeing anyone."

"Did she ever mention a man named Reynold to you?" Walt raised an eyebrow.

Daniel coughed as if he might have inhaled some of his coffee. "Reynold?"

"Yes. Did you know him?"

"Uh, I don't think so."

"So, she never mentioned him to you?" Samantha twirled her cup between her palms.

"No. Like I said, we weren't very close. Was she dating him?"

"I don't know about dating. I think they were just friends." Samantha shrugged. "He found her, you know."

"How morbid." Daniel shuddered. "I'd rather not talk about that."

Samantha glanced over at Walt. Walt met her eyes. It didn't take a genius detective to figure out that Daniel was lying. The question was, why?

Chapter Eight

"We need to move fast, who knows when they will get back."

"I'm aware, Eddy." Jo shot him a look. "I work best in silence."

"Okay, sorry."

She reached into her pocket and pulled out a long, thin knife. She began to wedge it between the window sash and the windowsill. Eddy leaned over her shoulder and peered at the windowsill.

"Don't do it that way, you'll leave a mark."

"Are you serious?" She looked over at him. "Who has experience here?"

"I've slipped into a few places in my time. That's low quality paint. Unless you want to leave evidence that you were here, you need to be careful."

She stared at him hard, then looked down at the paint. Small flakes of paint were peeled back so she had to be careful not to make it worse. She sighed and went at the lock with a gentler touch. Once she had the lock open she eased the window open.

"Good job." Eddy nodded.

"Stay out here. I'm not going to take the chance of tripping over you."

"I'll be right here if you need me, Jo." He offered her a wide smile. Jo swung her leg over the windowsill and then climbed the rest of the way in. Once she was on the other side she took a look around the living room. There wasn't much to see. Sparse furnishings, a carpet that should have been replaced years ago, and the faint scent of cat. She cringed at the thought. Cats could be very dangerous during a break-in. She spotted the ball of fur curled up on one of the couch cushions in the living room. She was fairly certain that it hadn't moved in hours. Still, she reminded herself to be cautious.

Against one of the walls in the living room was

a large, old fashioned roll up desk. If Daniel had any important documents he likely hid them in there. She walked up to it as quietly as she could so as not to rouse the cat. She was relieved to find that it wasn't locked when she tried to open it.

Inside was a messy pile of papers and envelopes. It was going to take some time to get through all of it. It wasn't as if she expected to find a piece of paper that detailed his plan to murder his sister, but there might be something to hint at that desire. Perhaps a letter to a friend, or a list of ways to kill someone. When she got down to the bottom of the pile she found a large brown envelope. She pulled it out and looked over the front. It was addressed to a lawyer's office.

Jo pulled out the papers that were tucked inside the envelope. From the content of the letter she surmised that the lawyer dealt with estate planning. The letter instructed the lawyer to review the enclosed documents for the proof that he had requested. She looked through the remainder of the papers. With each new document she became more certain of what Daniel was up to. Each paper involved another doctor's opinion of May's mental status. None of them were favorable. He even included a few testimonies from people that might have been friends of May, that insisted she'd begun to lose her memory quite often. Inside were also some power-of-attorney forms that hadn't been completed. It was clear to Jo that Daniel's intention was to get May's financial power-of-attorney or have her declared mentally incompetent so that he could have control of her finances. Jo snapped a few pictures of the documents then set the envelope back down on the desk.

Why was Daniel trying so hard to get control of May's finances? Was he angry with her? Was he just planning for the future? Did he decide to kill her instead?

Jo began to rummage a little further through the desk. She came across a leather bound book. She opened it to see names and numbers. The numbers had dollar signs next to them. It looked like some sort of transaction record keeping. Jo began photographing the pages starting from the end. She had only photographed a few pages when her cell phone vibrated in her pocket. When she checked it she saw a message from Eddy that Samantha was on her way back with Daniel. She made sure everything was back in place, then closed the desk. It bothered her that she didn't find out more information, but she didn't want to risk being arrested for breaking and entering. When she launched herself back out through the window she nearly landed on Eddy, who in a futile attempt to assist her, had reached up to steady her. He stumbled back when one of her feet struck him in the stomach.

"Watch it, Jo!"

"You're in my way, Eddy," she growled and grabbed his arm to catch him. "We don't need to draw any unneeded attention."

"I was just trying to help."

"I don't need your help."

"We need to stop arguing and get out of here."

"That, I can agree with." She gave him a light shove towards the car. As they reached the car Jo heard Samantha's car pull into the driveway.

"Get down." She tugged Eddy low.

"Why? They can't see us."

"We think they can't, but you never know. What if he walks this way? What if one of his neighbors decides to stroll over for a conversation? Better safe than sorry."

Eddy sighed and huddled beside her. "My knees aren't designed for this."

"Stop that." She rolled her eyes.

"What?"

"Acting as if you're so very old. Eddy, that's the only way you get old, acting like it."

"Okay, then my knees aren't screaming in pain."

"I told you to come to yoga with me, it will

help."

"I'm not wearing one of those leotards."

"What?" Jo laughed out loud then clamped her hand over her mouth. However, her shoulders still shook with the force of her laughter in reaction to the thought of Eddy in a leotard. "Plenty of men do yoga, Eddy."

"Maybe they do, but not this one. I earned these bum knees."

"Okay, suit yourself. Be old. But I can tell you that Samantha isn't."

"What does that mean?"

"I'm just saying." She straightened up. "We should be clear, let's head out."

"Wait, why did you say that about Samantha?"

"Never mind, old man, can you see well enough to drive?"

"Oh, you're asking for it, Jo."

"Am I?" She smiled at him. "I'm not scared.

With those knees you could never catch me."

"Hm. Yoga might be a good idea after all."

"I thought you might come round." She grinned. As they drove back to Samantha's villa she gave him an update on what she had found. "It isn't much. We already knew that Daniel had problems with his sister."

"I know. But the fact that he was trying so hard to get control of her finances indicates that he was up to something. It only makes him even more likely to be our suspect," Eddy said.

"Does it?" Jo rested her head on her fist as she looked out through the window. "Why would he go to all the trouble of plotting against her if he intended to kill her?"

"Maybe the plot didn't work, so he took an easier way out."

"I don't know." Jo frowned. "It doesn't add up to me. If he wanted her dead, he would have just killed her. It takes a lot of effort to get control over someone's finances."

"So maybe someone turned up the pressure on him, one of his debt collectors," Eddy said.

"Maybe. I guess we could look into that angle." Jo nodded.

"If you give Walt the pictures of the notebook you found he might be able to make some sense of them."

"I will."

"I managed to get some of Daniel's and May's financial records from my contact in the department and I've sent them to Walt. I'm sure that Walt will be able to trace his debtors and Samantha will be able to track them down."

"Yes, you're right," Jo said.

"You agree?"

"I do." Jo looked over at him. "Why wouldn't I?"

"I thought maybe you didn't have much faith in our abilities, since you decided to handle the situation with May on your own when she asked

77

you for help."

Jo was silent as she stared out through the windshield. It wasn't until the car rocked to a stop at a red light that she spoke.

"It's not like that at all."

"Okay." He pressed on the gas pedal as the light turned green. "What is it then? You just needed a break from us?"

"Eddy, you're all retired. You have a stable income that you can expect to live on for the rest of your lives. I don't have that. There are no retirement plans for thieves."

"I figured you had some money stashed away."

"I bet. I do. Some. But it's not going to last forever. I need to make more, while I can, before I can't."

"I see what you're saying. Still, we could have helped."

"If I'm going to try to make a go of this as a

business, then I need to be able to do things for myself. I can't afford to split the profit, and I can't expect you to work for free."

"Sure you can. We're retired. What else are we going to do with our time?" Eddy chuckled.

"Ha, if only that was true."

"All I'm saying is we're your friends. Any one of us would have been glad to help you."

"Okay. Thank you."

He pulled his car into the driveway of Samantha's villa and turned off the ignition. "Looks like they beat us here."

"With the way Samantha drives I'm not surprised." Jo laughed.

"Yes, she is a bit speedy, isn't she?"

"At times."

They walked up to the front door and right into a spat between Samantha and Walt.

"You can't base a hunch on something like that," Walt said.

"Why can't I?"

"Because you need something to back it up."

"It's a hunch, I don't need to back that up."

"Okay, okay." Jo held up her hands. "What is this about?"

"At the coffee shop Daniel acted as if he was financially sound, not his sister. We all know that's a lie. So that means he is probably lying about other things, too," Samantha said.

"A lie about finances does not make him a murderer." Walt shook his head.

"It might though. Especially if he makes a habit out of lying." Jo sat down on the arm of Samantha's couch. "It looks like Daniel was up to no good and attempting to get his sister declared mentally incompetent so that he could control her finances."

"With the way he spoke about her that doesn't surprise me." Samantha frowned. "Even after she's dead, he's still trying to convince people that she was a financial failure."

"Okay. Wait a minute. We don't know that she wasn't." Walt crossed his arms. "All we know for sure is that Daniel was accused of fraud. Maybe his sister was involved. Maybe she has made other bad financial decisions. I'm going to look into both of their finances including the documents Eddy got for me and see what I can find out."

"Good idea." Samantha nodded.

After a long discussion about the information they'd found, Samantha said goodbye to her friends. She was just about to close the door when she remembered that she needed bread. Without it she wouldn't be able to make the chicken sandwich she'd been looking forward to all day. As tired as she was, she decided to head back out to pick up a loaf of bread. On her way to her car she noticed Valerie walking down the street. The closer she got to Samantha the more Samantha had to fight the urge to ask her questions about May. She didn't have to fight for long, as Valerie walked right up to her.

"Samantha, I was hoping to catch you at

home."

"Oh?" Samantha turned to face her. "Why is that?"

"I heard that you and Walt had breakfast with Daniel, May's brother, this morning."

"Just coffee. How did you hear that?"

"How was he? Poor guy. Or is he? I mean I've heard some rumors that he might be a suspect. Do you think that's true?" She pulled out her phone and checked it, then tucked it back in her purse.

"I don't know. We just wanted to offer our sympathies for his loss."

"Please Samantha, I happen to know, that you and your little clique are always in the know when it comes to what is happening around Sage Gardens."

"I'm not sure why you think that. I would like to know how you found out about us having coffee with Daniel, though."

She pulled out her phone and checked it

again, then looked back at Samantha. "Word spreads, you know that. Anyway, I'd better be going."

"Wait, I have a question for you, Valerie."

"What is it?"

"Were you and May still at odds when she died?"

"I don't like to speak negatively about the dead." She glanced at her phone, then up at Samantha.

"So, you didn't patch things up?"

"I don't know, Samantha." She glanced at her phone again. "You know how sensitive May was."

"I didn't think she was sensitive at all."

"Well, maybe you didn't know her as well as you thought."

Samantha clenched her teeth to hold back the words that burned on the tip of her tongue. Valerie shrugged and checked her cell phone for what seemed like the thousandth time. Samantha guessed that she was waiting for a call.

"Valerie, I just want to know if you and May were still at odds."

"Why? What do you care? If you want me to tell you that I feel guilty that she died while we were still on the outs then fine, I will tell you. I do feel guilty. I wish I never said the things I did to her. But we were in a bit of a friendly rivalry and she was the one who criticized the decorations I put together for the Halloween party, remember?"

"I thought the decorations were great."

"I agree. But May said they were distasteful and creepy. It's Halloween! Anyway, that started the whole thing. I'm sorry she's gone, and I'm sorry that we didn't get along while she was here. But no, I don't harbor any bad feelings for May. The poor woman certainly didn't deserve what she got."

"No, she didn't." Samantha sighed and balled her hands into fists. "Whoever did it is going to be caught."

"Maybe. But if the police don't move quick, it's not likely to be solved, is it?" She raised an eyebrow. "At least that's what all of the television shows I watch seem to say."

"I'm sure it will be solved." Samantha locked eyes with her. "May deserves justice."

"Yes, of course she does. Bye now." She turned and walked away. Samantha stared after her. No matter how many times she talked to Valerie she was always left feeling a little confused. One moment she liked the woman, the next she didn't, then she liked her again. She was a hard person to pin down. As she climbed into the car and drove to the store she thought about what Valerie had said. Was it true? As the days ticked by would it be harder to find out the truth about May's death?

Chapter Nine

Walt settled behind his computer. He tried not to be distracted with thoughts of Jo. The more he got to know her, the more he wanted to make her life easier. She'd had a rough start, and life seemed to still be treating her harsher than most.

Walt logged into a financial search engine and began wiggling his way through Daniel's finances. He compared the information he found with some of the financial records that Eddy had given him. Right away Walt noticed a thread. Daniel had existed on credit and borrowed money for as far back as Walt could access. From what Samantha had found out it was probably since he got involved in the pyramid scheme. His credit rating steadily declined while his debt grew. He noticed that there were a few debt collection companies listed on Daniel's credit report. He traced that information down to discover the source of the debts. He found that Daniel borrowed from some less than reputable people, and they would have been determined to get their money back. At the time of May's death Daniel had a negative balance in his account, and almost all of his credit cards were maxed out.

"No wonder he was so determined to sell the property. He wouldn't last much longer on such a small retirement fund," he muttered to himself.

Then Walt looked at Daniel's most recent financial statements to see if there were any strange purchases. He didn't find anything unusual. Then he turned his attention to May. As he dug through her financial history he saw a much more responsible pattern of behavior. However, at one point during her brief marriage she depleted her funds to nearly nothing. As he moved forward in her life he found times when a certain amount of money left her account and showed up in her brother's account. It appeared she had been lending money to Daniel for some time. At least until the last year, when she moved into Sage Gardens. The rent for her villa stretched her budget more than before and there was no extra money to lend to Daniel.

"So, his cash cow was cut off, and she stood in the way of him making a good chunk of change from the property."

He shook his head and carried both May's and Daniel's financial records and a highlighter out onto the porch of his villa. In the late afternoon light he went through every single purchase. Most he could easily identify as routine purchases. He highlighted those that he had questions about, as well as cash withdrawals that were not part of a normal monthly pattern. By the time he was done Daniel's paper had plenty of yellow marks, while May's only had one. It was a cash withdrawal for one thousand dollars. It was an unusually large amount for her to take out. Walt tapped the highlighter against the paper and stared at the withdrawal for a long moment. It was only a few days before May's death. It crossed his mind that Samantha might be able to help him with this particular problem. He picked up his phone and dialed Samantha's number.

"Hello?"

"Samantha, can you get into the cameras at a bank?"

"I have a contact that might be able to, depending on what system they use."

"Could you see if they can crack into an ATM camera?"

"Do you think you found something?"

"I'm not sure yet. May made an unusual withdrawal from the ATM, and I'd just like to see if she was perhaps visibly upset. I'm trying to pinpoint what the money could have been for."

"Give me the bank and branch. Do you have the time and date?"

He supplied her the information.

"I'll call you back," Samantha said.

Walt waited patiently. Samantha had ways of getting information that surprised him, but he also didn't want to know how she got it.

After a few minutes she called him back.

"Walt, I have the information." She sighed. "But it can't be right."

"What? Is it the wrong branch maybe?"

"No, it's the right branch. But, it's not May."

"Who is it?"

"Hold on, I'm going to send you the still shot. Let's see if you think it's the same person I think it is."

Walt pulled the phone away from his ear as it beeped. He looked at the picture she sent in a text. Though the quality wasn't perfect there was no doubt in his mind.

"Daniel."

"Yes, that's what I thought, too. He must have had her ATM card."

"I wonder if May even knew that he took the money out."

"No way to know for sure. But remember she did ask Jo to look into some things, including money going missing. Maybe the stolen money triggered her fear?"

"Maybe she never knew it was Daniel."

"She was obviously suspicious, but maybe she died without ever knowing how deeply her brother betrayed her." Samantha clucked her tongue.

"Unless he's the one that took her life. Then she knew."

"True."

"I'm going to keep following the money to see if there is anything else there."

"I've been trying to track down some of Daniel's friends and associates, but I haven't been able to find many. It seems that he has led quite a lonely life."

"Maybe his whole life really was affected from being involved in the pyramid scheme. That's enough to make him capable of murder I think."

"I agree. I'll let Eddy know what you found. If

you discover anything else, just let me know."

"Will do. Thanks Samantha." He hung up the phone and tried to track down exactly where that money went. It didn't appear that he had deposited it into his account. In fact, he didn't see any indication of where the money might have gone. Maybe he still had the cash on him. The thought made Walt disgusted, but he doubted that was the case. A man like Daniel didn't ever have too much money in his hands.

Walt decided to work his way through some of Daniel's debtors to see if any of his debts had recently been paid off. He didn't notice any. Then he looked at the list of transactions that Jo had photographed. On the day that he withdrew the money he made a notation that a payment was made to Brent Nice and from what he could see it had cut the amount by about a quarter. Maybe it was part of a debt he paid off. Walt wanted to see if Eddy knew anything about Brent Nice. He dialed Eddy's number.

"Hello Walt, what did you find?"

"Nothing good. It looks to me like Daniel recently stole or borrowed one thousand dollars from his sister's bank account and I think he paid it to a Brent Nice."

"Oh, Nice huh? He's a loan shark so it was probably a debt. That's not a good person to owe money to."

"Do you know a lot about him?"

"A little. He's anything but nice. He has a reputation for being rough, to the point of intimidating those that missed payments with threats of going to their job, or their home to settle things. I know he's roughed up a few of his customers. At one point someone tried to press charges against him, but he backed out before the ink was even dry."

"Thanks Eddy."

"You might want to ask Jo for more information."

"Jo? Why?"

"She dealt in stolen goods, Brent Nice was

known to be a pretty lucrative fence. She might have crossed paths with him, and might know more about him than me."

"Okay. I will. Thanks Eddy."

"You're welcome. See what she has to say. And don't tell her that I suggested you call her. She already thinks I treat her like a criminal."

"You could be a bit softer."

"No, actually I couldn't. My rough patches are the only things holding me together."

"Oh, I see." Walt laughed. "Bye Eddy."

"Goodbye Walt."

As Walt hung up he thought about what he had learned so far about Brent. Maybe he threatened Daniel to the point that he stole from his sister. Could Brent have threatened him enough to make Daniel kill his sister? Walt considered the idea and dialed Jo's number. She answered right away.

"Hi Walt. How are you?"

He smiled a little. She was the only one of his friends that he had called that day that asked how he was, instead of what he had found.

"I'm doing okay. I'm afraid I've run into a bit of a dead end. I wondered if you might be able to help me with it."

"Sure. What is it?"

"Brent Nice?"

"Why are you asking me?"

"I just thought, that maybe..."

"Eddy told you to call me, didn't he?"

"I don't think he meant anything by it, he just thought you might know more about Brent than he did."

"Of course he did. Unfortunately, he's right. Brent's been around a long time and I've dealt with him on and off. I guess you could say we were even friends at one point."

"Really? You were friends with him?"

"Not exactly. I created a connection with him

95

as a way to protect myself from his goons. He was not the type of person you ever wanted to cross, so I made sure he had no reason not to like me."

"That seems like an intelligent move."

"I thought so at the time."

"It looks like Daniel owed him some money."

"Oh, that's not good." Jo sighed. "If he missed a payment, then he might have faced some serious consequences."

"Enough reason to kill his sister and inherit the land?"

"It's possible. Brent is not someone that anyone wants to cross."

"Okay, I'll make a note of it. Are you doing okay?"

"Yes, I'm just having a little trouble grasping this. Everything points to the brother, but I feel like we might be focusing too hard on just one suspect," Jo said.

"He looks good for it."

"Yes he does, but looks can be deceiving. I'd like to learn a bit more about Reynold."

"Samantha seemed pretty convinced that he had nothing to do with it," Walt said.

"Maybe she's too close to him? He was there right at the time of the murder. Maybe he knew about the brother's financial troubles and decided that everyone would blame him?"

"I hadn't really thought about that. You could be right."

"I guess next time we meet up we can discuss it. As of now, I'm off the clock. I have a Pilates class. Want to come?"

"No thank you."

"Are you sure?"

"Sweat, people, germs, no I don't think so."

"Okay." She laughed. "Don't say I didn't offer."

After Walt hung up the phone he decided to do some digging into Reynold. Maybe there was more there to find than he realized.

Chapter Ten

The entire time that Samantha ate her sandwich she tried to think of anything other than Valerie and the creepy feeling that their last encounter left her with. It was as if Valerie was devoid of emotion. May, a person she'd seen nearly every day for at least a year was found murdered, and Valerie barely batted an eye. That was so strange to her, and yet, she couldn't pinpoint why.

It wasn't until she finished the last bite of her sandwich, without having even taken the time to enjoy it, that it dawned on her. Valerie was a very dramatic person. Everything she did was surrounded by dramatic effect. The outfits she chose, the way she spoke to others, even the way she walked, all drew attention. But when it came to May's death she was surprisingly calm, as if it was just a bit of bad weather. It was a total shift in her personality. That was why it left her so unsettled. So what was with the turn around? Maybe she was dialing it back out of guilt. Maybe she regretted fighting with May and wanted to keep the attention off herself for once. But Samantha doubted that.

Samantha carried her plate to the sink to wash it. With each swipe of the cloth her mind grew clearer about Valerie. She had been acting very odd. As she listed in her mind all of Valerie's strange behavior she paced back and forth through the living room. On one hand she wanted to believe that Valerie had nothing to do with May's death. On the other, something didn't add up. The medical examiner had indicated that the attacker might be small or female. Valerie was petite, so it could have been her.

Samantha couldn't picture the woman with a fire poker in her grasp with the intent to murder. But was that because she preferred not to think of it as a possibility? She was tempted to call Eddy and discuss her suspicions with him, but she wasn't sure that he would share them. He might find the very notion to be ridiculous. In the end she decided to head to bed and think about it again in the morning. However, before she could make it to her bed her cell phone rang. She noticed it was Eddy and answered.

"What are you up to?" Samantha asked.

"It looks like we have our killer."

"Oh? Who?"

"Daniel. Just as we suspected. He stole money from his sister, one thousand dollars right before she died, and he was in debt with a violent loan shark. He had motive, opportunity, and I'm sure he did it."

"You're so sure that he did, but have the police reached the same conclusion? Are the police going to arrest him?"

"Not just yet. The detective on the case is moving very slow. I'm not sure why. I've heard rumors that he's the cautious type, but this crime seems pretty cut and dry to me."

"Maybe he knows something we don't?"

Samantha suggested.

"I suppose it's possible. We still don't know where Daniel was at the time of the murder. Maybe he has an alibi."

"If he does then we might have to rethink our suspicions."

"I'll see what I can find out. What are you doing?"

"Going to bed."

"What? This early?"

"I'm tired. I haven't been sleeping well."

"I'm sorry to hear that. Is there a reason why?"

"I'm not sure. I've been having some strange dreams I guess, and then all of this with May, I think I'm just a little worn out."

"You're not getting sick are you? Maybe you should pay Owen a visit."

"No, I don't think I need to do that. Once all of this settles I'm sure I'll be fine."

"Well, then let's hope that we can get it settled fast. I'll see what I can do to speed things along."

"Good luck, Eddy."

"Goodnight, Sam."

Samantha stretched out in her bed and looked up at the ceiling. She hoped that Eddy was right and they would find an answer soon. As she fell asleep her mind drifted back to the moments that she had shared with May. She had enjoyed spending time with her and they had had a budding friendship. As always Samantha needed to find out the truth. She fell asleep thinking about how she would discover that truth.

***

Eddy wearily wiped a hand across his face. All evening and late into the night he'd been working the theory that Daniel was to blame for his sister's death. After confirming with one of his police contacts that Daniel had no alibi for the morning of the murder, he was even more convinced. However, as he staged and acted out the crime scene for himself, he realized there were a few things that just didn't make sense. How did Daniel know that May would be in the community center? If she told him she planned to meet Reynold, why would he risk being caught by choosing to kill her there? The questions plagued him so intensely that he had to go outside and roam.

In the silence of the middle of the night, the beauty of Sage Gardens was hard to miss. Towering trees, lush well-tended grass, a sparkling blue lake, and bountiful gardens all reminded him that he lived in an amazing place. Except, for May it hadn't turned out that way. Without intending to, he ended up outside Samantha's villa. He recalled that she said she wasn't sleeping well. He hesitated to wake her up. But he really wanted to get her opinion on the matter. If there was anyone he trusted to talk him through a hunch, it was Samantha. He knocked once on the door. When he received no response, he crept around the side of the villa. Her bedroom curtain was open, though he'd reminded her hundreds of times to close it. She had argued that there was nothing for anyone to see as she closed it while getting changed or got changed in the bathroom. She liked to be woken by the sunlight that poured in through it.

"Samantha." He spoke loud enough to be heard through the thick glass. Samantha lay still in her bed. "Samantha." He tapped on her window again. He saw her shift in her bed. Then she lifted her head. She looked around the room for a moment, then finally towards the window. When she saw him, she let out a yelp and shied back. "Sh!" Eddy rolled his eyes. "Come to the front door."

Samantha nodded and climbed out of bed. Eddy shuffled around through the grass to the front door. With a quick glance in both directions for anyone watching he huddled by the front door. She opened it and clutched her robe around her.

"Eddy, it's midnight. What are you doing here?"

"Can I come in?" He met her eyes.

"Sure." She stepped back to allow him inside. With one hand she rubbed her eyes and with the other she pushed the door shut. "What are you doing here?"

"I had a thought."

"You had a thought?" She stared at him. "You woke me up in the middle of the night because you had a thought?"

"I woke you up because I'm afraid that it won't make sense to me in the morning. I just need someone to talk it through with. When I was a detective this was how I worked on every hunch I had. But I always had a partner to bounce my ideas off."

"At midnight?"

"Sometimes, yes." He frowned. "I can go if you want me to, I probably should."

"No, it's okay." She smiled at him. "Stay. Tell me about this hunch while I make us some tea."

He sighed and sat down on the couch. "I know we've been so hyper-focused on Daniel that we haven't properly investigated other suspects. But that article that was in the fire had nothing to do with Daniel. Why would she burn that article, or why would Daniel, if that had nothing to do with the murder?"

"Maybe it has something to do with the murder and we just don't know what yet. I mean, we don't know everything that went on between siblings."

"You're right, but I do know one thing. If he wanted to kill her, he could have done so at his house, or in her villa, or anytime that he took her out for dinner. Why would he go to all of the trouble of killing her in the community center? He didn't even bring his own murder weapon." He shook his head. "That doesn't sound like a premeditated murder to me. The more I think about it the more I think that Daniel had a plan to cause May harm, but I don't think it was to kill her. What I can't get out of my head is that he didn't need to. He managed to get doctors and friends to lie for him or at least convinced them that she was mentally unstable, so that he would get control of his parents' estate. He was a few steps away from seizing all of her assets. Why would he take it a step further and actually kill her when he could have gotten just as much by getting control of her finances?"

"You're right." Samantha pulled the kettle off the stove before it would shriek and wake the neighbors. She poured them each a steaming cup of tea, then turned back to Eddy. "I've been thinking about that part of it, too. It just doesn't add up. Even if he killed her in a fit of rage, why would he do it with a fire poker? He was much bigger and stronger than May, he could have easily overpowered her. It just seems like something that someone who was perhaps a bit weaker would do. Or maybe, someone who panicked. Daniel doesn't strike me as the type who panics."

"But if it wasn't Daniel, then who?" Eddy

shook his head. "I'd almost rather believe that it was Daniel because if it's not, we've spent an awful lot of time on the wrong suspect. We're practically back to square one."

"I don't think so. We still have other suspects to consider."

"Like who?"

"Well, May didn't exactly have a friendly relationship with Valerie. In fact, they were on the outs when May died. Apparently, May made some comment about the way that Valerie decorated the Halloween party, and I guess it brewed from there."

"You think someone killed her over Halloween decorations?"

"There may be more to it than that. I don't know. Valerie and May just really seemed to have something against each other."

"Still, that doesn't seem like much motive to go on."

"Maybe not."

"There's also Reynold."

"You still think he might be a suspect?"

"Yes, I do. I think there's a very good chance, since he was there and knew she would be there, and has since acted quite strangely."

"I think I would act pretty strange if my friend ended up with a fire poker in her chest." Samantha handed him his cup of tea. "But you may be right about considering him a suspect. We can't rule him out, that's for sure. Still, I think the key is that article. We need to find out more about the brothers who were mentioned in it."

"I just feel that there is something that I'm missing, something that's staring me right in the face, and all I have to do is blink to recognize it. I just can't get myself to blink."

"Maybe you need to sleep. Drink your tea. It will help you relax." Samantha had a sip of her tea and yawned.

"I can't sleep. I have too much energy. I'm just not going to be able to sleep until this case is over." Eddy sipped his tea.

A few minutes later Samantha pulled a spare blanket over him on the couch. He snored loud enough to make her jump. She rolled her eyes and gathered their cups to put in the sink. By the time she made it back to her bed her entire body ached from exhaustion. Once there, she collapsed. Her dreams were peppered with the loud snores of her guest.

Chapter Eleven

Just when Samantha settled into what she hoped was a sound sleep a knock on the door woke her. She blinked and noticed that the sun was up. She must have slept a bit longer than she thought. But who was at the door? She stumbled into the living room amid Eddy's snoring. It certainly wasn't him at the door. She trudged across the living room with sleep still heavy on her muscles. She hadn't slept well in the past few days, but the night before was the worst. She tugged open the door and peered outside into the morning sun.

"Jo?"

"Hey Samantha. Are you okay? Are you sick?"

"Hm? No, I'm not sick. Why?"

"You're still in your pajamas."

"Oh." Samantha yawned and shook her head. "I had a late night."

"I see. I can come back later if you want."

"No, it's fine. Come inside. Just don't sit on Eddy."

"Huh?" Jo stepped inside the villa and spotted the lump on the couch. "He slept here last night?"

"Slept, I suppose, all I know for sure is that he certainly snored." She yawned again. "So, what brings you here?" Jo continued to stare at Eddy on the couch.

"I didn't know things were so serious between you two."

"What?" Samantha laughed and waved her hand at her. "He showed up at my door at midnight with a hunch. That's all it was. Please, like we're in high school or something."

Jo shrugged and smiled a little. "I don't feel much different than I did then to be honest. Anyway, enough of that. I just came from the café down the road and the waitress that works there told me that she saw May and Daniel arguing. She said that it got so heated she almost had to ask

113

them to leave."

"What were they arguing about?"

"He kept insisting that they had to sell the property, she kept insisting that they didn't. She wanted it to stay in the family, and go to a younger cousin. He didn't like that idea at all. But the argument got really bad when they started talking about someone named Jacob."

"Jacob?" Samantha finally fully woke up. "Why were they arguing about him?"

"The waitress told me that May said something about Reynold looking just like Jacob, and that they could easily be twins, and something about a scar. She didn't hear what else she said, but Daniel shouted at May that she was senile, stood up and stalked out of the restaurant."

"There it is!" Samantha waved her fist in the air. "There it is! The connection!"

Eddy snored loudly, then sat straight up. "Where am I?" He stared at the two women. "What is going on here?"

"Relax Eddy, you fell asleep on my couch."

"Oh." Eddy blinked, then rubbed his forehead. "So, what's all the noise about?"

"Jo found the connection between Reynold, our victim and the man in the article, Jacob."

"What connection?"

"Somehow, May knew Jacob, the man mentioned in the article, that drowned, remember? May said that Reynold looked just like him, could have been his twin."

"Oh yes. Okay." He yawned and struggled to focus.

"From the conversation it seems that Daniel knew Jacob, too. So that means that there's a good chance that article that burned in the fire, had more to do with May's death than any argument over some property."

"A chance." Jo nodded. "But the way the waitress described the argument I'd say Daniel had plenty of animosity towards his sister. Apparently he said that a scar means nothing and

115

that she was going senile."

"Do you think Reynold and Daniel were friends as well? Maybe Reynold was in on the murder. He could have lured May to the community center so that Daniel could kill her," Samantha said.

Eddy shook his head. "No, that doesn't make sense. Why would he want to kill her there, in a public place, instead of in her villa?"

"I'm not sure what to think just yet." Samantha tapped her chin. "But we need to find out more about Jacob's death as soon as possible. It seems to be relevant and there is some sort of secret that surrounds it, and when we figure it out, we might just crack the case."

"If there is a case file I'll see if I can get my police contact to get it from Mariner County. It should have the names of everyone involved. It'll also contain any inconsistencies found in the exam of the body if there are any. A lot of times a detective will tuck in little bits and pieces of information that maybe he didn't follow up on, or didn't pan out. So, there might be something there."

"Even for an accidental drowning?" Samantha asked.

"It depends on how much of an investigation they did." He rubbed his eyes, then stretched his arms above his head. "I'll call Chris as soon as I get home." He glanced at Samantha. "Thanks for the couch."

"You're welcome, Eddy."

He nodded to both of the women, then walked out of the villa. As soon as the door was closed, Jo settled her gaze on Samantha. Samantha rolled her eyes and did her best to change the subject.

"So, if May took the time to print out the article about Jacob's death, then she had to know something about him or his family that made the event personal to her."

"Yes. The fact that she knew what Jacob looked like, despite the fact that the article didn't include a picture, could indicate that she knew Jacob."

"It's been a very long time since his death."

"Something that the waitress told me really sticks out in my mind. May said Reynold could be Jacob's twin. The article said that Jacob was out fishing with his brother. Brothers can look pretty similar sometimes."

"Yes, they can. But the article said that Jacob's brother on the boat was John."

"Maybe it's another brother then?"

"Maybe," Samantha nodded. "So, a man May knew dies several years ago. Then his brother shows up at Sage Gardens. May is reminded of Jacob's death and talks to her brother about it?"

"But why?"

"I don't know. My best guess is that if the conversation inspired that much anger from Daniel perhaps there is something about Jacob's death that Daniel doesn't want exposed."

"Interesting." Jo nodded.

"We may not be just looking at solving one mystery here, we might be looking at solving two."

Chapter Twelve

Eddy still felt sluggish as he hung up the phone with the lab tech he knew at the police department. Chris assured him he would get the files sent over as soon as possible. He hoped that meant within a few hours and not within a few weeks. He sat down in his large recliner and closed his eyes. One by one the suspects paraded through his mind. Daniel with his desire to gain control of his sister's finances. Reynold at the crime scene, with a mystery hanging over his head. Then there was Valerie. At first he dismissed Samantha's suggestion that Valerie could be involved, but the more he thought about it the more he wondered if she might be right. Just because she seemed harmless, and didn't appear to have a direct connection to the crime didn't mean that she couldn't be involved.

Eddy decided that he would take a walk down to the tennis courts and see if she was there. He'd noticed her there a few times in the past, and hoped that he might be lucky. When he spotted her in the middle of a game he suddenly recognized what the connection might be. Her partner across the net was Reynold. Eddy stood back outside the fenced court and watched as the two played. From the way they communicated and played with each other it appeared as if it wasn't their first game. When the ball sailed past Valerie she huffed and put her hands on her hips.

"That was out!"

"It was inside the line, Valerie."

"Reynold, if I say it was out, then it was out."

"Okay fine, it was out. Just get the ball."

Eddy narrowed his eyes. Were they bickering with each other?

"Hey, Eddy!" Reynold waved to him as Valerie jogged back onto the court with the ball.

"Eddy's here?" Valerie shielded her eyes with her hand and looked through the fence.

"Just admiring the match. You two are pretty good."

"Thanks." Valerie smiled and twirled her tennis skirt. "It's a great way to stay fit."

"I see that." Eddy chuckled.

"Watch it now, Eddy." Valerie winked at him. "Or Reynold might get jealous."

"Oh really?" Eddy held up his hands. "Sorry Reynold, I didn't know you two were together."

"We're not."

"Don't be shy, Reynold." Valerie giggled. "We're just not official yet."

"I see. Well, your secret is safe with me. How are you holding up, Reynold?"

"I'm still a little shaken up. I'll be better when they figure out who did this."

"Oh absolutely." Valerie wrapped her arm around Reynold's shoulders. "This poor fellow had quite a shock. All because he tried to be a good friend."

"Is that so?" Eddy zeroed in on Valerie.

"Yes, I mean, if he'd never agreed to meet with her that morning he wouldn't have walked into such a horrific scene."

"Valerie please, I'd rather not rehash it."

"Don't be so modest, Reynold. She called you so upset and you jumped right up to be there for her. Too bad it was too late."

"Yes, too bad." He stared down at the tennis court. "I wish I'd gotten there just a little sooner."

"I'm sure. We all wish we'd known, and could have protected May, Reynold. You're not alone in that," Eddy said.

"But it just wasn't meant to be." Valerie squeezed his shoulders. "So, now we just have to move forward. Don't we, Reynold?"

"Sure." Reynold shrugged off her grasp. "We should get back to our game. We only reserved the court for an hour."

"Oh absolutely. I didn't mean to be a

distraction." Eddy waved to them and started to walk away. He paused after a few steps and turned back. "So Reynold, you two didn't plan to meet for a friendly cup of coffee? It was a last minute thing?"

"Sort of. She called me the night before upset about something and I offered to take her out to coffee."

"Oh okay." Eddy nodded and continued to walk away. Thoughts jumped in all directions within his mind. Valerie and Reynold were dating? May was upset when she agreed to meet Reynold for coffee? None of it made sense at the moment, but he had a feeling that it all would soon enough. When Eddy made it back to his villa, he was still deep in thought. His cell phone rang so loud that he jumped. He sighed and shook his head. It was easy to disrupt him when he was concentrating on something so hard. He kept trying to fit the pieces of the case together. While there was a lot of overlap, he couldn't get it to work out just right in his mind. He noticed the phone call was from Chris.

"I've managed to get a copy of the file you wanted."

"Thanks. I'll be right in to get it."

"It's already in your mailbox."

"How did you do that so quickly?"

"Magic."

"Thanks Chris."

After going to his mailbox to pick up the file Eddy sat at his kitchen table to go through it. He flipped the file open and began to read through the details of the death. Even though Jacob's death was ruled accidental an inquiry was opened before the ruling was made. Jacob was on a fishing trip with his brother, John. They were drinking, but not to excess according to the investigator. Jacob fell overboard in an attempt to retrieve a fishing pole that he had dropped in the water. Since he was a very good swimmer John assumed that he would resurface and didn't attempt to rescue his brother. John claimed that he thought his brother might be playing a joke on him, and still didn't attempt to rescue him. It wasn't until he realized how long it had been, that he jumped into the water. When he couldn't find him, he rowed to shore to get help.

The rescue mission was classified as recovery by the time the rescue response began. Eddy read over the details again. Then a third time. There was no mention of anyone else being on the water with Jacob and John. There was no sign of foul play. Jacob's body was found with his foot tangled in branches under the water. The medical examiner ruled it an accidental drowning.

Eddy sat back in his chair and closed his eyes for a moment. He tried to picture the two brothers out on the boat. Were they out there to blow off steam? There's a cooler, beers on ice, mosquitoes in the air, it's muggy. He took a deep breath. The water is murky, but still. The fishing lines plop right into the water. What went wrong? He attempted to pick up the fishing pole. Did one brother bump into the other? Did the boat list for some reason? Did someone drop their bottle of beer? Or could they have argued? No matter what caused it, one brother ended up at the bottom of the lake. Was it possible that John knew that Jacob wasn't coming back up? Did he push him out of the boat?

Eddy flipped to the witness's section of the file. There was only one name listed. But that one name was enough to make his heart drop. John Reynold Smith. Everything seemed to suddenly fall into place. Reynold must go by his middle name. Reynold was Jacob's brother? Reynold was the other person in the boat with him? Now that was a connection. He pulled out his phone and called Samantha.

"Are you free?"

"I can be, for you."

"Great. I want to have a conversation with Reynold."

"Oh? Do you want me to meet you?"

"No, I'll come pick you up."

"Great, I'll be ready."

Samantha hung up the phone and frowned. She'd heard Eddy sound that way before. It usually meant that he was on to something. But why did it involve Reynold? She reminded herself that she had to find a way to be objective. Reynold was a suspect, even if her instincts told her otherwise.

Chapter Thirteen

Samantha made sure she was ready to go when Eddy pulled up at her villa. She went outside and a few minutes later when he arrived she climbed into his car.

"What's going on? I know that you found out something."

"Oh yes, I found out two things actually." He started to drive.

"Well?" She stared at him.

"I'll tell you soon."

"Huh? No, I want you to tell me now."

"Not right now, I'm driving."

Samantha continued to stare at him. "We talk all of the time while you're driving. What did you find out?"

"Just be patient, Samantha. I'd rather wait until after we talk to Reynold to tell you."

"Why?"

"Because."

"You don't trust me?"

"I have my reasons."

"Would you please just tell me?"

"Samantha, anyone ever told you that you are infuriating?"

"Yes, many times, mostly you. That doesn't answer my question."

"You don't trust me?" Eddy asked. "I told you, I have my reasons." He parked in Reynold's driveway, just behind his car.

"Okay. I guess." She sighed and stepped out of the car.

"You knock." He pointed to the door.

"Why?"

"Samantha!"

"All right, all right." She hurried up to the door and knocked. After a few minutes Reynold

130

opened the door.

"Samantha hello. How can I help you?"

Samantha stared at him blankly. She had no idea why she was there. "I just wanted to check in with you. I know it was such a shock to find May that way. Are you doing okay?"

"Yes, I'm managing."

"With Valerie's help right?" Eddy stepped up beside Samantha.

"What? Oh, Eddy, I didn't see you there."

"Wanted to check on you too, Reynold."

"But we just saw each other this morning."

"Right, when you were with Valerie."

"Right." He lowered his eyes. "What is this about?"

Samantha could only study Reynold's face as she had no idea why they were there. She noticed that his cheeks flushed, and his lips tightened as Eddy stepped closer to him.

"I'm sorry, I had no idea that this is the second

tragic death you've witnessed," Eddy said.

"I don't know what you're talking about." He started to step back into the house. "You've checked on me, now I need to get some things done."

"Wait a minute. I just wanted to say, I'm sorry about what happened to your brother."

"I don't want to talk about that." He started to close the door. Samantha slipped a foot into the door before he could.

"It's okay, John." Eddy noticed his eyes widen slightly. As he looked at them Eddy noticed a scar above his left eye. Eddy thought that maybe that was the scar May was talking about. "We're here to listen. Is there anything that you want to tell us?"

"Samantha, kindly remove your foot before I close the door on it. I've had enough of your good wishes. Please, just leave me in peace."

Samantha stepped back and glanced over at Eddy. "He's right, Eddy. We've bothered him enough."

Eddy nodded and followed her down the driveway back to his car. Once inside, he backed down the driveway.

"Okay spill. What was all of that about? Reynold is dating Valerie? What was that business about his brother?"

"Yes, Reynold is dating Valerie, and Reynold is also Jacob Smith's brother. The one that was in the boat with him when he drowned. Reynold's full name is John Reynold Smith. It looks like he goes by his middle name now."

"From the article?" Samantha's mouth hung open. "Wait, wait. That means that when May said that Reynold looked just like Jacob, she was talking about the man that drowned and John. They were brothers. But did she know that?"

"I'm not sure. However, I suspect that Daniel might be able to answer that. Why don't we take a spin by his house?"

"We could do that." Samantha nodded. "Why

didn't you tell me about all of this before we spoke to Reynold?"

"I didn't want you to know because I wanted you to be able to see his expressions clearly."

"Well, I did. For one, he didn't want anyone knowing that he was dating Valerie, and for two, he didn't want to speak a word about his brother. He is definitely hiding something."

"Yes, I agree. But I wanted you to see for yourself. If you knew what I did, it would have been harder for you to gauge what his reaction was like."

"I understand."

"I also noticed that he had a scar on his left eyebrow. Do you think that was what May was referring to?"

"Maybe, but lots of people have scars."

"True."

"I think it's time we call a meeting and figure out our next step. Even though Reynold might be involved, this certainly doesn't eliminate Daniel as a suspect. In fact if he is somehow connected to Jacob's death, or May is, that makes him even more of a central suspect. The question is who did May print out the article for, Daniel or Reynold?"

"Or maybe, who had the most reason to want that article eliminated, along with the person who printed it."

Samantha sent a text to Jo.

Update, meet at my house.

She duplicated the text to Walt's number.

Once everyone arrived Eddy filled them in on the information they'd discovered. Samantha set out a bowl of pretzels and a pitcher of ice water along with some cups. As her friends gathered around the table she couldn't help but think of May. If only she had asked her more questions about why she wanted to find the article.

In the end there was no way to predict what would happen. Or perhaps May had. Perhaps she sensed danger, and thought the safest place would be with Reynold. It still wrenched her heart to think that Reynold might have been the murderer, even as she comforted him. However, something even darker surfaced in her mind. What if it wasn't Reynold or Daniel at all?

"I wouldn't put it past Valerie to be jealous enough to go after May," Samantha said.

"Just because she was meeting with Reynold?" Walt asked.

"She strikes me as a very possessive person," Samantha said.

"But enough to kill?" Jo picked up the pitcher and poured a glass of water. "Are they even serious?"

"I think she is a bit more serious than he is." Eddy grabbed a handful of pretzels. "The way she talked wasn't exactly reflected in the way he behaved. In fact, he seemed a bit annoyed."

"And even more annoyed when I found out about it." Samantha sat down at the table. "I thought she was acting a little off, but now that I know she's involved with Reynold, and Reynold is somehow involved in all of this, I suspect her even more. However, it's still hard to believe that she would go so far as to kill May."

"The problem is we have three prime suspects, and all of them have motive, all of them have opportunity," Walt said.

"Wait a minute, the only person who actually knew that May would be at the community center was Reynold. Daniel didn't know. Valerie didn't know," Jo said.

"Valerie might have known. Reynold might have told her. And it's possible that May told Daniel where she would be. Maybe she said that she intended to confront Reynold with the information they knew when they met for coffee that morning," Walt said.

"Maybe." Samantha pursed her lips. There was something on the edge of her mind that she knew was important. "How did they get in?"

"What do you mean? Wasn't the door

unlocked?"

"It shouldn't have been. It was too early for it to be open. Don't you think?"

"I never really thought about that." Jo narrowed her eyes. "It was a bit early for the doors to be open."

"But Valerie is on the decorating committee, which means that she has a key," Samantha said. "I still have one from when I helped with the trivia night last month."

"You think she opened the door?" Jo said.

"Maybe May planned to meet Reynold outside like Reynold said, but found the door open, and went inside. Maybe Valerie was waiting for her."

"That makes sense." Walt nodded. "If the door was cracked open, May might have been inquisitive enough to look inside."

"But again, if she planned all of this out, why would she do it in such a public place, and why wouldn't she be prepared with a more convenient murder weapon," Jo said.

"What we need is a single piece of evidence that points us in the right direction." Eddy shook his head. "The problem is, we're running out of places to find that evidence. We already checked Daniel's house and other than the financial issues, he was clean. Nothing to show that he wanted to harm his sister, nothing to show that he knows anything about Jacob's death that he would want to cover up."

"We didn't check his car!" Samantha snapped her fingers. "Maybe the evidence is in there. Remember? We took my car when we went for coffee. He even said that we couldn't take his."

"Yes, that's true." Walt frowned. "But what could we find in his car?"

"Who knows! If he was trying to hide things, maybe he would keep them out of his house. He had to know the police would question and investigate him when his sister was killed," Samantha said. "So, maybe he stowed whatever incriminating evidence he has in the car to hide it. When I was actively reporting I always lived out of my car. It's the one thing that we overlooked."

"I did." Jo nodded. "You're right. I had the perfect opportunity, too, as he was already gone. I'm sorry that I didn't think of it."

"Jo, please don't apologize, you did everything you were supposed to and got us lots of information." Walt cringed. "I hate to think of what might have been living in your car right along with you, Samantha."

"Me too." Samantha laughed. "Looking back on it now, it definitely grosses me out. It's worth a shot. It might hold that one piece of evidence that we need."

"Okay, then it's settled, we'll go take a look at his car." Jo smiled. "It will only take me a few seconds to get in."

"No." Eddy shook his head. "We're not going to break into it."

"Why not?" Jo glanced over at him.

"Because there are other ways we can get in. We can't always fall back on the same bad habit to get information."

"Bad habit?" Jo crossed her arms. "Do you really want to go down that road?"

"I don't mean it that way, Jo, you know I don't. Try not to be so defensive."

"Considering I'm the only one that's spent time in prison, I think it's fair for me to be a little defensive."

"She's right." Walt nodded. "Jo has more at risk than the rest of us."

"That's clear, but my point is, we're engaging in risky behavior when we don't need to. I don't want any of us to end up behind bars, least of all Jo. If we take some time to consider it, I'm sure there's a ploy that we can use to get into the car without having to break in. What do you think? Can we make more of an effort to make things legal and less risky?" Eddy said.

"I'm all for it." Walt nodded.

"It will take a lot longer." Jo sighed.

Samantha looked around at her friends and knew that all of them were waiting to hear her opinion on the situation. She took a deep breath and looked into Eddy's eyes. "I think Eddy is right. We are treading awfully close to being just as criminal as the criminals we talk about. After all, we don't know for certain that Daniel is the murderer, and we have already broken into his home. So, if we can come up with a viable plan that will give us a look around his car, I think we owe it to ourselves to give it a shot. Otherwise we may begin to lose ourselves, lose our moral compass."

"Moral compass?" Jo laughed.

"Stop." Walt narrowed his eyes. "We all have morals, otherwise we wouldn't be trying to do this for May. Jo, you left that life behind you, and we shouldn't be encouraging you to relive it, when we can just as easily work together to prevent you from being put in that position."

"I've heard this routine before." Jo pursed her lips as she looked at Walt. "I know what you really think of me, Walt, and I appreciate how much you care. But this is a silly argument, over breaking into a car. I will handle it."

"No." Eddy locked eyes with her. "The answer is no. We're not breaking into it."

"Sure Eddy, boss, whatever you say." Jo stood up and saluted him.

"Jo, don't be upset. We're only trying to do things right," Eddy said.

"Well then, I guess you don't need the ex-con around." She turned towards the door and without another word walked out of the villa.

Samantha frowned. "Eddy, look what you did."

"Me? You agreed with me."

"Because I was trying to be supportive."

"I still say I'm right." He sat back in his chair. "If we're going to be Jo's friends we shouldn't be leaning on her every time the law needs to be broken."

"I'm sure she'll be fine once we figure out how to get into the car without breaking in. I'm going to head home and think about it," Walt said.

"I'm going to look into Valerie a little more. Eddy, could you see if she's had any run-ins with the law as well? If she really is crazy enough to have killed May out of jealousy, I bet this isn't the first time that she's done something irrational."

"Good point. Sure, I'll look into it." Eddy lingered as Walt left the villa. Once he and Samantha were alone he looked over at her.

"Did you really just agree with me to support me?"

"Yes." She shrugged. "Jo has certain talents, I don't think there's anything wrong with her using them."

"Then you should have said that. Why would you lie for me?"

"It wasn't really a lie. I do support your

144

opinion, I just don't think it's up to us to make the choice for Jo. If she didn't want to do it, she could have said no."

"Still, I don't want you to hide how you feel. Why would you? Did you think I would get mad?"

"No." She smiled as she met his eyes. "Nothing about you scares me, Eddy. I just felt it was the right thing to show some loyalty, that's all."

"Loyalty." He raised an eyebrow.

"You're my friend, Eddy. I don't want to argue with you over everything. I can trust that sometimes with your background you might know a little better about certain things."

"Interesting. I'll have to keep that in mind. I'll let you know if I find out anything about Valerie."

"Okay, thanks." She nodded to him as she held open the door for him. Once he left she closed the door and sighed. She sent Jo a quick text about the situation, but when she didn't get a response she settled down at the computer. She began to search through Valerie's social media accounts for links with John Reynold Smith, Jacob Smith, as well as Daniel Ewan and May Ewan. She found quite a few pictures with both Valerie and May that were posted in the last couple of years. There was also one with May and Daniel. At first Samantha almost skipped right past it, but something made her go back and look again. As she thought, Daniel and Valerie were holding hands in the photograph. Did Valerie have a thing with Daniel as well? She shook her head at the idea, but printed the photograph to refer back to.

As she dug deeper into Valerie's past she couldn't find any further connection. From what she could tell she never lived in the same cities as any of the other three, she didn't attend the same schools. She couldn't find a single thing that tied them all together, aside from Sage Gardens. She knew that since May and Valerie had been friends at one point there was a chance that she'd gotten to know Daniel. Unfortunately, the only way to know for sure was to either ask Valerie or Daniel and she doubted that either was going to be very forthcoming with an answer. She decided since she had a little time she would still make an effort. First she attempted to call Valerie. However, her phone went straight to voicemail.

"Hi Valerie, it's Samantha. I just had something I wanted to talk with you about. You know, girl talk. Call me back if you get a chance. Thanks!" She hung up the phone and wondered if she had poured on the sugar a little too heavily. Would Valerie be able to tell that she was up to something just from her overly sweet tone of voice? She cleared her throat and decided to exercise a little more caution with Daniel. She dialed his number, fully prepared to hear another voicemail message. Instead he answered the phone.

"Hi Samantha." She was so surprised to hear his voice that she didn't answer at first. "This is Samantha, isn't it?"

"Yes, it is, I'm sorry. I had something caught

147

in my throat."

"Oh wow, that's not good, are you all right?"

"Yes, I am now."

"Good. Glad to hear that. I'm also glad that you called."

"You are?"

"Sure, I've been waiting for this call."

"What do you mean?"

"I sensed a connection between us when we went out for coffee. I know that you sensed it, too. So, I figured it would just be a matter of time before you decided to call. You held out longer than I expected."

"Oh yes, of course. I wasn't sure if you'd felt that, too."

"Yes, I did. It's quite strong. We have some very serious chemistry between us. So the question is, what are we going to do about that?"

"I just thought we could get to know each other a little better. I suppose I hesitated to call because I wasn't sure if you were a free man. You're not seeing anyone are you?"

"Not at the moment, but we can change that. Can't we?"

"I suppose we could." She laughed. "I wonder if there is a place we could meet to chat?"

"Why don't you come to my place?"

Samantha's heart dropped. Even though she was confident in her ability to protect herself she didn't exactly want to put herself in such a vulnerable position. If she did she might not be able to get back out of it.

"I was thinking somewhere more central. Say, the library?"

"The library? That's an odd date, but if it's what you want that's fine with me."

"Do you want to pick me up on the way?" Samantha thought it was the perfect opportunity to get a look inside his car.

"No, I think I'll meet you there. When do you

want me to be there?"

"In twenty minutes?"

"Wow, you really don't want to wait." He laughed again. "I can't say that I blame you, I'm ready to get this going, too. I'll be there."

"Great." Samantha gritted her teeth to hold back her disgust. Sure, Daniel might not have been a killer, but he was still a man who was horrible to his sister. "I'll see you there." After she hung up the phone, she wondered if she'd made the right choice. Was it a good idea to be anywhere alone with Daniel? If he was the murderer he might take any opportunity to get rid of a person he deemed a risk. With these thoughts fueling her fear she considered calling Eddy to have him tag along with her. But she suspected the moment that Daniel got wind of this not being a friendly visit he would clam up and not admit to anything. She needed to do this on her own, even if that left her a little on edge.

Chapter Fourteen

When Samantha arrived at the library she found that it was pretty crowded for mid-day. It didn't take long for her to discover why. One of the residents from the Sage Garden's poetry group that May had belonged to was hosting a poetry reading in honor of May. The moment she realized this her heartbeat quickened. How would Daniel react? It didn't take long to find out, as he was seated at a table not far from the poetry reading. She paused for a moment beside a large pillar to watch his reaction to the words that strangers read about his sister. His attention was focused on the woman at the podium, however his expression was not somber. In fact, as she watched his lips curved upward with a subtle twitch. He reached up and spread his hand across his mouth, perhaps to disguise laughter.

Samantha told herself that she had to be imagining it. No man, even if he had been the one to commit the crime, could be amused by his sister's death. Could he? She walked towards the table with a heavy feeling in her chest. Could she even have a casual conversation with him when all she wanted to do was reach across the table and shake him?

"Samantha." He stood up and smiled as she approached him. "I'm glad you asked to meet."

"Me too." Samantha bit into her bottom lip as he pulled out a chair for her and she sat down in it.

"I felt like we didn't get much of a chance to talk over coffee. There's so much I'd like to know about you."

"Really?" She tilted her head to the side. "Why is that?"

"Oh, May spoke very highly of you. I didn't put two and two together when we went for coffee, but then I remembered that May had said that you had an illustrious career as a crime journalist."

"I'm not sure I'd describe it quite like that."

She smiled.

"Well, she did. She was quite impressed that a woman could do so well for herself, I suppose since May didn't ever do much more than run a cash register."

"May was very intelligent. And creative."

"Sure." He shrugged. "Anyway, why did you want to meet at a library?"

"There are some things I'd like to talk to you about and I thought the library would be nice and quiet so we could do that."

"What did you want to talk about?"

"I noticed that you and Valerie were rather close. I didn't know if that was still something that was true since I happened to see her with someone else."

"Valerie?" He blinked, then shook his head. "I'm not sure I know who you mean."

"She's a resident at Sage Gardens, too. A friend of May's?"

"Oh, Val, right. Yes, I met her one of the last times I visited. She's a very friendly gal. A little too friendly if you know what I mean. We went out to dinner one night and then it was like she expected me to marry her. Anyway, I let her down as easy as I could and we haven't seen each other since. So no, you don't have anything to worry about. I'm a free man." He winked at her.

"That's good to know." She resisted a glare. "I suppose after May's death you'll need a little time to heal."

"Not really. Actually, I can finally plan for the future. Once May's estate is handled I can start my life again."

"May's death benefits you?"

"Absolutely. Look, like I told the cops, I didn't kill her, but I sure wanted to. She was holding the inheritance our parents left us as ransom, and wouldn't even help me out with my bills anymore. I was drowning. Now that she's gone I can settle my debts and move on with my life."

"Don't you hear how horrible that sounds? To talk about your sister's death that way?" Samantha stared at him, too shocked to even be angry.

"Maybe you didn't know my sister very well. Look, when we were growing up she was always the golden child. She could do no wrong. My parents adored her, the community adored her, everyone believed that she'd be this great success. I was constantly having to prove myself to even get a little attention. When we became adults it was the same thing. She got her college paid for, just because I didn't want to go to college, I didn't get anything. I got tangled up in something that I was too young and too stupid to understand was a scam. Instead of her being there for me and helping me out, since she had such an advantage over me, she did nothing to help me, she made me take a deal. No loyalty, at all."

"You were involved in a scam, maybe she thought she was protecting you?"

"No, all she cared about was her reputation.

She didn't want anyone to find out that her brother was a criminal. So, she forced me to take a deal and turn on my partners, so I wouldn't get convicted. Ever since then I've had to look over my shoulder."

"That must have been rough for you."

"It still is. I can't wait to just disappear. As soon as I get my hands on that money, I can get away, far away, and I won't have to worry anymore. I never had the chance to live my life, you know? All because of one mistake that I made well over thirty years ago."

"Yes, that's rough." She swallowed back harsh words. As long as he thought she had sympathy for him he would keep talking. "I'm sure she lorded her success over you, too."

"She tried, but I didn't buy it. It's not success to work in a retail store, no matter what position you're in. She wasted her education, and my parents knew it before they died, but they still treated her like their little princess."

"Always in her shadow, I can see how that would drive you crazy."

"It did, I'll admit it. But I just focused on taking care of myself."

"Still, you came to visit her."

"Well, family is family." He shrugged. "She was all I had left, so I tried to connect with her. But she didn't make it easy. So, sorry if I'm not falling to pieces over her being gone, but it is what it is, right?"

"Right. It's better to be honest than to pretend that you're brokenhearted."

"That's what I think, too, but you'd be surprised by how many people don't agree with that. Every other question is about the funeral and my plans for her headstone, and so on. As if I'm really supposed to be concerned about that."

"You're not planning a funeral?"

"Graveside service, it was the cheapest I could get."

Samantha's stomach churned. "She deserves more than that."

"She's dead. She's not going to care how she's laid to rest."

"Don't you think that she deserves better? That she might know somehow?"

"You mean like she's peering over pearly white clouds down at the rest of us poor souls?" He chuckled. "No Samantha, I'm sorry. I don't buy into any of that. Even if I did, if Heaven was real, trust me the last thing she's going to do is look back down on this miserable life."

"Daniel, that sounds like your opinion, not hers."

"My life hasn't been that miserable. I've lived it, for the good, for the bad. But she didn't take a single risk. She never took a chance, never took a risk. What kind of life is that?"

"I don't know, she seemed pretty happy to me."

"Simple minded." He rolled his eyes.

"Anyway, that's not what we're here to talk about, is it?"

"Actually, I don't remember why I came here at all."

"Because you feel what I feel, we have chemistry." He reached out and took her hand in his. "No need to fight it."

She pulled her hand back and glared at him. "Oh trust me, it's not a fight. Anyone who could feel that way about his sister is not someone that I want to get to know better." She stood up from the table.

"Then why did you ask me here?" He glared up at her. "Was this some kind of joke for you? Some kind of trick?"

"Look Daniel, I truly hope that one day you realize that your sister deserves to be treated better." Samantha's cheeks blazed as she realized that everyone in the library, including those there for the poetry reading, stared at her.

Daniel stood up from his chair and pointed a

finger at her. "You conned me didn't you? You just wanted to get more information out of me for your little detective game, huh? Well, get all the information you want, I didn't kill my sister and nothing that you can do will change that."

He stormed past her and out of the library. Samantha stared back at those that stared at her. As she slowly turned away it dawned on her that she'd just put herself in a terrible position. Now, not only did Daniel know that she suspected him, but so did the library that was mainly filled with Sage Gardens residents. Which meant that in no time at all Reynold and Valerie would know about her little blow up as well. The investigation they worked so hard on was about to collapse, all because she lost her temper. As she hurried out of the library she tried not to think of what Daniel might be planning. He could claim to be innocent all he wanted, but she didn't believe him, not for a second.

***

By the time Samantha reached her villa her

nerves were on edge. She decided to walk around the lake trying to calm herself. She prided herself on being able to keep her cool, but in that moment it wasn't possible. All she could think about was the way Daniel spoke about May. No one deserved to be treated like that, no matter the history. She was still wound up, but decided to go to her villa and try to distract herself by doing more research.

As Samantha opened the door to her villa her cell phone began to ring. She ignored it. She knew it was either Eddy, or any number of Sage Gardens residents that had heard about the library incident. She closed the door behind her and wondered how she was going to explain herself. She was just about to sit down at the computer when there was a knock on the door. She turned around just as the door opened. Eddy stuck his head inside.

"Your phone is ringing."

"I know it is."

"So?" He held up his phone and ended the

call. "Is there a reason you're not answering?"

"You know the reason, Eddy." She sighed.

"Yes, I heard about it."

"And?"

"And?"

"I don't know why I lost it."

"I do, Daniel is a horrible person and you couldn't stand being around him."

"But I might have just ruined everything."

"No, you didn't." He crossed the living room to her. "You've got things stirred up for sure, but you didn't ruin anything. Did you find out any information?"

"I found a photograph with Daniel and Valerie holding hands. When I saw it I decided to ask him myself if he dated Valerie. According to him it wasn't much more than a fling, but Valerie expected a lot more."

"You think that gave her motive to kill May?"

"I don't see why it would, to be honest.

However, the way Daniel talked about May makes me even more certain that he'd have no problem with killing her. I really think he's our guy."

"All right, just take a breath. It's easy to jump to conclusions when you're angry."

"Eddy, he practically told me that he was glad that she was dead. How can that be anything but the words of a murderer?"

"Samantha, it's quite suspicious, but do you really think that if he was the killer he would talk like that? It would make him the prime suspect."

"And it has. Maybe he's just that arrogant. Or maybe he thinks that it will throw the police off his scent, just like it has thrown you off his scent." She crossed her arms.

"Now wait a minute, Samantha, it hasn't thrown me off anything. All I'm saying is that it's too soon to pick one horse and sometimes when emotions run high it's easy to make assumptions."

"My emotions are not running high."

"Sam." He looked into her eyes "You know I

know you."

"Ugh, fine, okay." She turned away. "I might be a little wound up. But you would be too if you had to hear those slimy words come out of his mouth."

"You shouldn't have met up with him."

"I wanted him to talk, and he did." She frowned. "Now we know that Valerie dated both of our main suspects. What does that tell us?"

"That I might be the only person Valerie hasn't dated?" Eddy chuckled.

"I'm serious, Eddy. The question is, was it a coincidence, or did she know that there was some kind of connection between Daniel and Reynold?"

"That is a good question. It leads us back to the same thing. We need to see if we can get any real evidence on Daniel. Once we do we might be able to pinpoint one suspect."

"We could already have that evidence if we hadn't argued with Jo," Samantha said.

"Don't start about that, please."

"Why shouldn't I?" Samantha raised an eyebrow. Before Eddy could reply there was a knock on the door. Samantha used the moment to break the tension between them. She pulled open the door to find Walt on the other side with a smile that spread from ear to ear.

"I came up with a plan." Walt strode proudly inside. "Look." He held up a coupon. "I made this myself on the computer. It's a coupon for one free car detailing, today only. I'm going to make sure that Daniel gets it, so that we can take a look around the inside of his car."

"Oh great job, Walt. This looks really real." Samantha studied it. "Do you think he will go for it?"

"I think we can certainly try." Walt nodded. "I know I like free things. I don't think I would be able to turn this down."

"As if your car has a speck of dirt in it."

"It never hurts to give it a little extra shine."

He grinned.

"What do you think, Eddy?" Samantha showed him the coupon.

"I think we should have let Jo do what she needed to do. I don't know why I was so stubborn with her." He sighed.

"You worry about her." Samantha patted his shoulder. "One day she'll appreciate that. Besides, Walt has come up with a great idea, and we might not need her to break in after all. Maybe you were right all along."

"Maybe."

"So, no to the coupon?" Walt look disappointed.

"We can give it a shot. But you guys will have to stay out of sight when we get his car because he knows your faces," Eddy said.

"I hadn't thought of that. Good thinking, Eddy," Walt said.

"Why don't we go stick it under his door?

That's a good way to make sure that he gets it," Eddy said.

"Good idea." Samantha grabbed her keys from the counter. "I'll drive."

"Oh, well, uh." Walt cleared his throat.

"Walt, you rode in my car once and survived."

"I know, and I don't think I packed enough wet wipes to do it again."

"Walt!" Samantha exclaimed.

"Let's just take Walt's car." Eddy smiled. "I've been in your car too, Sam."

"Eddy." Samantha rolled her eyes and stuck an elbow in his side. "Those are your taco wrappers on the floor you know."

"I know." Eddy laughed.

As they piled into Walt's car Samantha tried not to touch anything. She knew that Walt would give the car a thorough cleaning once they were out, anyway. It was just Walt's way. She tried not to let it offend her. As they drove towards Daniel's house, Eddy tilted his head back towards where Samantha sat in the backseat.

"So, Daniel and May lived in the same town as Reynold and Jacob at one point. However, not at the time of Jacob's death. It doesn't exactly explain how they knew each other. Were they friends? Neighbors?"

"Still, they have to be connected to May's murder somehow." Samantha's eyes widened.

"I'm not sure how. I can't find any motive for it. The only bad blood I came across was between siblings," Eddy said.

"Maybe there's more to it than that. We'll have to dig a little deeper. Who knows, Valerie might be the key to us figuring all of this out. Maybe she knows what their connection is."

"It might be worth a conversation with her," Eddy said.

"Considering the way that I blew things up with Daniel today, I'm sure that if the two are working together somehow, he's already contacted her." Samantha leaned her head against the side window.

"Maybe, but you said that he claimed he didn't have anything going with her. He might not have called her," Eddy said.

"If he was telling the truth."

"That's a big if." Walt turned his car down the street that led to Daniel's house.

Chapter Fifteen

Jo walked up to Daniel's car. She had no interest in being told what to do. She'd grown to respect Eddy, Walt and Samantha, but when it came to breaking and entering she saw no reason to hum and haw. If there was evidence in the car a simple pop open of the car door would tell her everything that she needed to know. In and out in no longer than a minute, and she would redeem herself. It bugged her that she hadn't thought about the car in the first place.

Once Jo was beside the car she glanced around to see if any neighbors were out watering the grass or if there were kids on skateboards. When she didn't see anything she looked towards the house. The curtains were pulled tight and the door was closed. There was no music or noise drifting out from any potentially open windows. Sure, Daniel was home, but he was likely totally oblivious to the fact that a stranger stood in his driveway.

Jo pulled a thin, flat tool out of her pocket and began to slide it into the lock, however the moment she touched the handle she realized it had plenty of give. It seemed to her that the car wasn't even locked. She smiled to herself. It wasn't exactly breaking and entering if the door was unlocked. She lifted the handle to open the door in the same moment that someone shouted her name.

"Jo! No!" Walt lunged towards her from the bottom of the driveway. Jo stared at him for a brief moment before she heard the click. Her eyes widened and she ran straight for the bottom of the driveway. Walt tackled her onto the front lawn just as the explosion filled the air. He held her down in the dirt with his body splayed over hers. Samantha shouted for them as she ran towards them. Eddy had his phone out to call for help. Jo spit out a few pieces of grass and wondered if she was still alive. Walt's weight on top of her informed her that she likely was.

"Are you okay?" His voice struggled to reach her. She could barely hear. What happened? Her ears rung with the force of the explosion. Walt slid off her and she pushed herself up to her knees. The car that she had almost sat down in was nothing but rubble. Even the corner of the roof had been impacted by the force of the explosion. Her eyes watered with the realization that she could have been ash if it wasn't for Walt distracting her. She would have sat down in that much faster than the time it took for the bomb to go off. Was it a bomb?

"Walt?" She stared at him. His face was covered in a mixture of soot and dirt. He looked so different when he wasn't sparkling clean.

"It's okay. We're okay. Everyone's okay." Walt offered her his hand to help her to her feet.

"Are you sure?" Eddy grabbed Jo's elbow and looked her over. "You aren't hurt?" His eyes surveyed her from head to toe.

"Eddy, it's okay. I'm okay." She looked into

his eyes. "I'm okay."

Eddy took a deep breath and looked back towards the car. As he did the front door of the house flew open and Daniel ran out in nothing but his boxers. His hair was wet as if he might have just taken a shower.

"What is going on here?" He glared across the lawn at Samantha and Walt. "You two again? Did you do this?"

"No, we didn't." Walt held up his hand, but shuddered when he saw the amount of dirt on it. "Oh no, oh dear." He rummaged in his pocket for some tissues.

"Eddy, what should we do?" Samantha frowned. "He's going to have a lot of questions."

Eddy narrowed his eyes. "Jo, you need to get out of here before the police arrive. There's no need for you to be here."

"Are you sure?"

"I'm sure. Get in your car and go." He tilted his head in the direction of the street. Jo didn't have to be told again, she took off towards her car.

"What about us?" Samantha glanced over at Daniel who stared at his car with disbelief. "Do we stay, or go?"

"Stay." Eddy stared at the scene. "The police are going to need an explanation and we can give them an eye witness account. But, in our version, I'm the one that opened the car door. We came to check on Daniel. Walt noticed the blinking under the car. I lifted the handle to see if it was rigged, and boom."

"Do you think they will buy that?" Samantha asked.

"They will have to if it's all that we tell them. Jo not being here won't change anything about the case, we're just going to have to stretch the truth a little."

"That's quite flexible of you, Eddy," Samantha said.

"I've learned a few things from you." He shot her a brief smile.

As a police car skidded to a stop in front of the residence followed by a firetruck, Samantha was glad that Eddy was there. He remained by her side throughout the police officer's questioning. Walt stammered through most of it. Samantha's ears rang so loud that she guessed Walt also had a hard time hearing the officer's questions clearly. By the time they were able to leave the scene, Samantha was exhausted. She didn't overlook the fact that Daniel shot her dirty looks every chance he got.

"I think Daniel really believes we had something to do with his car blowing up."

Eddy put a finger to his lips. "Sh, wait until we're clear of the crime scene."

Samantha nodded and followed him back to Walt's car. Walt wandered along beside them, almost as if he couldn't get his balance. Samantha noticed that his hands twitched at his sides, still streaked with dirt. She'd never seen Walt move so fast. When he spotted the blinking light and saw Jo approach the car, he was like a blur as he took off after her.

"Walt, are you okay?" She touched his back. He jumped in reaction to the touch and pulled away.

"I will be, Samantha. I'm just a little unnerved."

"I think we all are," Samantha said.

Eddy frowned and glanced back at the crime scene.

Once they were all inside the car Eddy looked into the backseat at Samantha. "What if he did it?"

"What do you mean?" Samantha asked.

"What if he's the one that rigged the car?"

"Daniel? Why would he do that?" She stared at him with wide eyes.

"I don't know, maybe you were right. Maybe there was evidence in the car that he couldn't get rid of, so he rigged the car to blow up when someone opened the door."

"Like the police?" Samantha shook her head. "Daniel may be crazy, but to attempt to kill a police officer? That's just asking for life in prison. He had no way of predicting who would try to lift the handle."

"Or maybe he did." Walt clutched the wheel tight as he drove. "Maybe he thought it would be you, Samantha, after your conversation at the library. Maybe he knew that you were suspicious so he wanted you to be eliminated."

"Maybe." Samantha shivered at the thought. After all, it could have just as easily been her, or any one of them, that opened the car door. "But it would be a huge stretch. He had no way of knowing for sure. Plus, there wasn't a lot of time between our conversation and when Jo opened that door. He would have had to make a decision to kill me, then decide how to do it, then make and plant the bomb."

"Not to mention that Jo's search didn't turn up any chemicals or unusual equipment in the house," Eddy said. "I'm sure she would have noticed if there were the makings of a bomb hanging around."

"True." Samantha nodded.

"Okay, so if we're sure that Daniel didn't do it, who did?" Walt squinted through the windshield. "Someone must have. The killer?"

"I have no idea." Samantha sighed. "Just when I start to think I have something figured out, a car blows up."

"It was almost Jo." Eddy lowered his eyes and grimaced.

"I know." Walt pulled the car into the driveway of Samantha's villa.

"If Walt wasn't there..." Samantha breathed out her words.

"I don't even want to think about it." Walt looked between his two friends. "I still can't believe that I managed to get to her in time. It wasn't likely, and yet I still tried."

"Shows how much you care." Eddy smiled. Samantha climbed out of the backseat. She reached up and rubbed one of her ears in an attempt to hear clearly.

"How long before all of this noise in my ears goes away?" Samantha asked.

"Could be a day, could be a few. If it keeps up after that you'll need to go to the doctor to get it checked out," Eddy said.

"Yes, I noticed a bit of a ringing in my ears, but it already went away for me." Walt turned towards his villa. "I'm going to head home and shower." He shuddered as he caught sight of a smudge of dirt on the back of his hand. Samantha waved to Walt as he drove away. Eddy followed her up to the door of her villa.

"If you're worried about your ears why don't you have Owen take a look?"

"I'm not sure that Owen would be able to tell anything. I'd probably have to go to the hospital. Besides, it may clear up soon. How are yours?" Samantha asked.

"A little fuzzy, but not too bad. It helps that my hearing is already going south."

"Is it really?" She unlocked her door and

glanced over at him. "I didn't know that."

"Nothing too serious yet, but let's just say that my old age has been confirmed."

"Eddy, you're not old." Samantha smiled and kissed his cheek. "Just weathered."

"Hm? Is that supposed to be some kind of compliment?"

"Yes." She pushed open her door. "You know, experienced, wise."

"It has nothing to do with my wrinkles?"

"What wrinkles?"

"Now, I think you should get your eyes checked out along with your ears."

Samantha laughed and tossed her purse down on the couch. "Believe what you want, Eddy, but you're the talk of Sage Gardens."

"Stop it." He rolled his eyes. "Even if that were true, I don't want to know about it. Besides, it's not what we should be thinking about now."

"You're right, I guess I was just trying to

distract myself." Samantha sat down on the couch and rubbed her fingertips along her forehead. "Do you think we're ever going to figure this out?"

"I'm just glad that Jo is okay."

"We think she's okay."

"You should probably go check on her," Eddy said.

"I think you should come with me to talk to her."

"Why?"

"Because it's the right thing to do, Eddy. She went off and did things on her own and obviously she thought we didn't trust her. All of this needs to be smoothed over. She's probably terrified, and having you there might help calm her down."

Eddy shook his head. "I don't think that Jo has ever been terrified by anything. She might be a little shaken up though."

"She's not superhuman. She's a person, and she almost got blown to smithereens. You don't think that's a good reason to reach out to her?"

Eddy looked into her eyes. "You're not going to let this go are you?"

"No, I'm not. There's no reason to. We need to go see her."

"Fine. All right, I'll go." He growled.

"How can you be this stubborn? I know you're more caring than this. Why is it so hard for you to go see her?"

"You really can't figure that out?" He snapped at her and then frowned. "I'm sorry. I didn't mean to speak so harshly. But can't you see why I don't want to go?"

"No, I can't. She's your friend. Our friend."

"A friend who wouldn't have been putting herself at risk if I hadn't been so pigheaded in the first place. It's my fault that she was there, alone. It's my fault that she thought she couldn't get back-up."

"Oh Eddy, you can't blame yourself for that.

Jo does what she does, no matter what anyone says. I'm sure she doesn't blame you. After all, we were there, even if by accident."

"I don't know, Samantha. I'm pretty mad at myself, so I would expect she would be mad at me, too."

"I don't think she will be. But we can't know whether she will be or not if we don't go. So what are you going to do, let her think you don't care, or show up even if she might be upset?"

"You're right." He nodded. "I'll go."

"Good." She looked at him. "Listen Eddy. Jo knows that you mean well. She knows that."

"I hope so."

Chapter Sixteen

As Samantha and Eddy walked towards Jo's villa, Eddy noticed that several people clustered around a make-shift memorial to May. His heart sank. In the middle of all of this chaos, they were still no closer to finding out who actually killed her. If it wasn't for Jo, their prime suspect would have gone up in smoke. Samantha was right. Why would he set a bomb to go off in his own car? Clearly, he wasn't the killer. Or at the very least, someone else was involved. It suddenly occurred to Eddy that when the blast filled the air it could have been any one of them with their hand on the door. Samantha knocked on the door then pushed it open, just in time to hear Jo protesting.

"I told you already, Walt, I'm fine. I wish you would just go home."

"I'm not going anywhere until we find out exactly what happened at Daniel's house."

"Well, that's not likely to happen anytime

soon. Hi Samantha, hi Eddy, sure come right inside, no need to be invited."

"Just here to check on you." Samantha smiled at her. "Walt, I thought you were going home?"

"I was, but I just couldn't. I needed to see Jo and make sure that she was safe, and that she didn't have any intentions to go after the perpetrator herself."

"It was a little explosion, not the end of the world. It happened, it's over, and I'm fine," Jo said.

Eddy kept his gaze averted.

"You might as well join the crowd." Jo rolled her eyes and gestured for them to come in. "I'm telling you all, I'm fine."

"I think after what we all went through today it's pretty normal to be concerned." Samantha tilted her head to the side. "None of us expected that to happen."

"Maybe, but I think we need less focus on me, and more focus on who planted that bomb."

"Well, like we said before, we don't think it was Daniel." Walt frowned.

"Unless he was trying to throw suspicion off himself." Samantha's eyes widened. "I guess it's possible."

"If that were the case he would have used a timer, not a trigger set for the door handle. Who else did he expect to try to open the car door?" Walt shook his head.

"That's a good point." Samantha tapped her chin. "So someone wanted Daniel dead. Who?"

"The actual murderer?" Jo sat down on the edge of the couch. "Maybe someone was after both May and Daniel, they are siblings after all. We've been focused on only May being the target, but maybe they both were."

"Still, someone who goes from using a fire poker to using a bomb, that's a big jump." Eddy pursed his lips in thought. "And, it requires skill. You can't just slap together a bomb. Whoever did this knew what they were doing."

"It sounds to me like we need to be thinking about the people he owes money to. Maybe when they realized they were never going to collect, they decided to take him out." Jo shrugged. "Bombs are more likely to be made by a loan shark than a retiree."

"So, you think it's possible that whoever planted the bomb actually had nothing to do with May's murder?"

"I think for a murderer to follow up their crime with a bomb, that's very unusual." Eddy frowned. "Nothing about this is fitting together the way it needs to. Maybe we just need to take a breath and give ourselves some time to review the information that we already have. If we do that something new might come to the surface."

"I think you're right." Walt nodded. "With the blast, we've probably all forgotten some important detail. A shock can erase even the most important memories."

"Then we'll meet in the morning to review?"

Eddy looked between his friends. "After breakfast, say about ten?"

"Yes, I'll be there." Jo nodded.

"Me too." Samantha yawned. "I could use a break."

"Where are we going to meet?" Walt pulled out his phone to make a note of it.

"How about in the community center? The scene of the original crime," Samantha suggested.

"Okay. Good plan," Walt said.

As the others left, Samantha lingered.

"What is it, Samantha?" Jo turned to face her with a steady stare. "I know there's something on your mind."

"Hm?"

"Don't act innocent, you're still here for a reason."

"I just need one thing from you, Jo, and then I'll go."

"What?" Jo raised an eyebrow. Samantha

held her arms wide open. Jo's eyes widened and then she embraced her, Samantha folded her arms around her. "All right, it was a little scary." Jo sighed.

"Which part? The part with the bomb or the part where Walt tackled you?"

Jo started laughing and she pulled away as she looked at Samantha. "I didn't think he had it in him."

"For you, he does." Samantha winked at her. Jo rolled her eyes.

"You're seeing things that aren't there."

"If you say so. Are you sure you're going to be okay by yourself?"

"Yes, to be honest, I need some time alone. I've had a little too much togetherness lately."

"Okay, but remember, safety comes in numbers. I know why you did what you did, and I know that it is important to you to work alone, but you need to be aware that we all have your back. You're not alone in any of this."

"I can admit that today taught me not to take my friends for granted. I know I make light of it, but the truth is that if Walt hadn't shown up the moment he did, I wouldn't have made it out of there alive. I can't even begin to think of a way to thank him, to thank the three of you for being there."

"You don't have to. It makes a big difference when we work as a team."

"And I went off and did something stupid on my own."

"It wasn't stupid. You were trying to solve the case. It was brave. None of us had any idea there was a bomb under that car."

"I wasn't exactly as cautious as I should have been."

"It's a wake-up call for all of us. We're not investigating a petty theft, we're investigating a murder, and we need to be very aware of our surroundings."

"You're right, Samantha." She stifled a yawn.

"Right now all I want to be aware of is my bed. I'll see you in the morning at the community center."

"I'll be there." Samantha gave her another quick hug.

As she walked back to her own villa she thought about the crime. There was a piece missing, something that linked all of the pieces in the chain, if she could just figure it out, everything would fall into place. However, when she reached her villa she decided to review some information about Valerie. Even though she was a possible suspect, Samantha hadn't done much research on her past. She had been blinded by the fact that she thought she knew her, and then distracted by the photograph she found of Valerie holding hands with Daniel.

Samantha settled at the computer and began to investigate the woman she thought she knew. As she dug deep into her past she discovered many broken hearts along the way. Valerie was not only engaged several times, she announced the engagement each time. Despite the many attempts, as far as Samantha could tell Valerie never actually married. Which meant she dealt with failed relationship, after failed relationship. Samantha felt a twinge of sympathy for the woman who clearly wanted that once in a lifetime love and struggled to find it.

Samantha dug further into Valerie's past, and was surprised to come across the fact that Valerie was in the military. It wasn't that unusual for a woman to be in the military, but Valerie never struck her as someone who could be that disciplined. She was an impeccable dresser, and always had her hair styled as if she'd just walked out of the salon. Appearance was important to her, and to picture her in a uniform or sweating through boot camp was almost impossible. It seemed the military wasn't the right fit as her career ended after ten years with a dishonorable discharge. Samantha tried to figure out why, but she couldn't find any clear reason. However, she did discover that Valerie was involved in explosives. Her heart dropped when it struck her that Valerie might have been the one to plant the bomb. Would she really do that? Anyone could have opened that door. So Valerie had the knowledge to plant the bomb, but what motive could she have? Did Daniel have something on her?

Samantha thought about paying Daniel another visit, but after the way he reacted to their presence at the time of the explosion, she didn't think that would be very effective. She picked up her phone to call Eddy and update him on what she had found out about Valerie, but before she could her cell phone began to ring. Walt's name flashed across the screen.

"Hi Walt, what did you find?"

"How did you know I found something?"

"You rarely call for no reason."

"True, that would be rather inconsiderate."

"What did you find, Walt?"

"I decided to do some digging into the loan sharks that Daniel owed money to. I wanted to see if any had a history of using explosives to get their point across. I came across something rather strange."

"What's that?"

"As you know I've looked into Reynold's financials, and also into Daniel's financials. Reynold's financials are spotless. However, I hadn't really looked into Jacob's financials."

"Jacob's? The one who drowned?"

"Yes. I didn't think there was much reason to look into him because I didn't think there would be anything about his financial records from so long ago and also Jacob was not a suspect, or a victim."

"As far as we know."

"Yes, I'm getting to that. Now, as I was looking into Daniel's history I discovered like you did that he got into debt many years ago. We assumed from what we found that he got into debt originally, shortly before Jacob's death around the time he was accused of fraud. So, I decided to look more into the court documents associated with the fraud. I've found our connection between Daniel, Reynold, and Jacob."

"What is it?" Samantha's eyes widened. She wished she could reach through the phone and shake the information out of Walt.

"You see, Samantha, in order for a pyramid scheme to work it's most important to have…"

"Walt! I know about pyramid schemes, please just tell me the connection."

"Oh dear, calm down, Samantha, you don't want to get your stress level up, that's a leading cause of many diseases and…"

"Walt!"

"Fine, fine. From what I can gather from the transcripts, Daniel pulled Jacob into the pyramid scheme with him, which led to them both taking loans to cover the debt that they created by over-investing in the scheme. So, not only did Daniel ruin himself financially, it seems he also played a big part in ruining Jacob financially."

"How interesting." Samantha narrowed her eyes. "So, perhaps May knew Reynold while her brother and Jacob were both involved in the pyramid scheme."

"Yes, and perhaps Reynold had a problem with Daniel because of what he did to his brother."

"Maybe, but Jacob died. So did his debts. Would that really be motivation to go after May?"

"I can't honestly say what would motivate a person to kill another person. But I do think it adds another dimension to this investigation. Suppose Jacob didn't die an accidental death. Suppose he jumped into the water on purpose."

"Suicide?"

"Maybe with all of the debt he faced he thought it was his only way out. If that was the case then Reynold might blame Daniel, and in turn May, for his brother's death."

"Wow, that is a sad thing to consider. I guess it could be possible. But I think if we're going to consider that Jacob's death might not have been accidental then maybe we should think about whether it might have been murder."

"Murder? How did you get from suicide to murder?" Walt sounded mystified.

"It's just something to think about. If we suspect that Reynold might have killed May, then we might want to consider that he might have also killed his brother on that fishing trip. Maybe he was embarrassed by his brother's debt, or maybe they argued about it."

"You're right, that is something to consider. Maybe Daniel or May found out about it and suspected Reynold, which would give him plenty of motive."

"Would you like to hear the dimension I can add?"

"Yes, please do."

"First, did you find any loan sharks with a history of using explosives?" Samantha asked.

"No, I didn't. I must say, I got a little distracted. I have put a list together for Eddy so

197

he can look into them further."

"I did find someone who is an expert in explosives. Valerie."

"What?" Walt asked.

"Yes, she did ten years in the military and specialized in explosives. I think it's safe to say that she could be responsible for the bomb planted on Daniel's car. However hard that is for me to imagine, she has the experience."

"But why would she do it? Do you think she had something against Daniel?"

"I think there are a few possibilities. One is she killed May and suspects that Daniel might know something about it. The second is that she is just trying to protect Reynold. And, since we know that she dated Daniel at one point and clearly has a history of chronic romance, maybe she wanted revenge for him dismissing her so easily."

"Hm interesting. I hadn't really thought about her as a murderer much, but if she can plant a bomb for the purpose of murder, I guess she could have also killed May. Hard to believe we could be living in the same place for so long with a killer in our midst," Walt said.

"I'll see if I can find out anything else about Jacob. Maybe there's some connection that we're overlooking. But at least now we know how Reynold, Daniel, May, and Jacob are all connected."

"At least we think we do. I suppose it's still possible that it's a coincidence and had nothing to do with the murder," Walt said.

"Maybe, but I don't think so. I hope we find something at the community center tomorrow, otherwise we might just be spinning our wheels."

"Don't give up hope now, Samantha, we're getting close, I can feel it."

"You can feel it?" Samantha laughed. "It's not like you to trust your intuition, Walt."

"I'm trying out new things."

"Good to know." Samantha hung up the

phone and began to consider what to do next. Now that she knew that Jacob was involved in the same scheme as Daniel, she wondered if Daniel might have somehow had something to do with Jacob's death. Maybe Daniel was in the water waiting for Jacob? Maybe Daniel and Reynold planned it together? None of it quite made sense to her. Perhaps that was because she was so tired. It was difficult for her to think when her mind swirled with exhaustion.

In surrender, she crawled into bed despite the early hour. She soon fell asleep, despite her mind whirring with suspects and facts.

Chapter Seventeen

When Samantha woke up, it was around eleven at night. The explosion from earlier in the day still rang in her ears. Her hearing was still muffled from the impact of the blast, but in her head she heard it loud and clear, as if it was stuck on repeat. The more she tried to go back to sleep, the more frustrated she became. What if someone was rigging up a bomb to one of their cars as they slept? It was a bit of a stretch to believe they would be targeted, but she just couldn't get it out of her head. What if May was the first, but others would follow? Daniel survived. Would the killer go after him again? The worst part was, she still suspected Daniel. As absurd as it was to still believe that he was a killer, she did.

After another toss and turn she sat up in bed. There was no point in trying to sleep. She considered calling Eddy to see if he was awake, but changed her mind. Maybe, just maybe, there would be something left in the fireplace, or something had rolled under the couch in the community room. There had to be some clue somewhere that would point them in the right direction. She dressed and walked down the sidewalk towards the community center.

Samantha was sure it would be locked, but she had the key from when she had helped with the trivia night. She decided to try the knob on the door before using her key. She was surprised when she found that it was unlocked. Her mind started to churn. Why would it be unlocked? Maybe the police had left it unlocked? Maybe someone was so distracted by what happened there that they forgot to lock it? She frowned and pulled the door open. Once inside she noticed that there was a light on in the kitchen. Her heart stopped beating for a moment. Was someone else in the building? She ducked down behind the couch and waited to find out.

Moments later a surprising sight greeted her. A woman, dressed all in white, with a strange glow around her, stepped out of one of the dark hallways and into the recreational area. Samantha couldn't see her face from her position. She held her breath as she remained hidden behind the couch. She'd never been one to believe in ghosts, but with the sight she'd just seen, she wondered if it might be May returning to ensure justice. She willed herself to peek around the side of the couch. As before she noticed the woman in a long robe with an eerie glow around her. A shiver raced up her spine. However, her rational mind took over and reminded her that this was a real person, who had no reason to be in the community room in the middle of the night. The question was, should she confront her, or just hope that she left on her own?

Samantha shifted her feet as her ankles ached from the crouched position she was in. When she did she heard a crunch. A leftover pretzel or cracker was trapped under one of her shoes. She froze and waited to see whether the woman would notice her. Footsteps shuffled in her direction.

Ghosts, didn't walk, they floated, she was fairly certain. She braced herself as she expected to be discovered. Then the footsteps stopped. The sound of the front door to the community center opening forced her to open her eyes. She could see an outline of what she guessed was a male figure. He walked in the direction of the woman.

"I told you no lights." He growled his words with enough authority that Samantha tensed in reaction to it.

"It's not a light, it's just a little glow stick. I didn't want to trip and break a hip or anything."

"Put it away. Even the slightest light could draw the wrong attention."

"Fine."

The eerie glow disappeared. Samantha didn't know whether to be relieved that she was right about ghosts, or terrified that two very real people were meeting in secret a few feet away from her.

"This whole thing is getting out of control," the man said.

"I know it is."

"You should have stayed out of this. If only May hadn't told you anything."

"But she did. I'm glad she did. I told you I would help."

"You haven't helped, you've only made things worse."

"That's what you see right now, but give it some time and it'll help in the long run."

"I wish May had never said a word to you about me."

"Please, don't be like that." She sighed. "I know that you have feelings for me."

"Stop that nonsense. Can't you see how foolish it is to even be thinking about that right now?"

"Is it really so foolish? I know this is bad timing, but it doesn't change what we share. How much longer do we have to hide it?"

"With everything going on, this is what you

want to talk about? It's not just bad timing, it's impossible timing. The first chance I get, I have to disappear."

"Then I'll disappear with you. I don't have any reason to stay," the woman said.

He sighed and began to pace. Samantha peered around the side of the couch. No matter how hard she tried she couldn't clearly see either of their faces. Because of the explosion earlier she had a difficult time hearing any specific qualities in their voices. She could make out most of their words, but didn't recognize who they were. If she could just get a closer look she was sure she would be able to find out who May's killer was.

"No, that's not going to happen. It's much easier to disappear alone than it is with another person. Look, I don't mean to hurt you but..."

"Don't!" The woman said.

"Keep your voice down!"

"You dare speak another word and I promise you that you will regret it. I'm not going to be treated like this."

"I think you have the wrong idea about what life on the run will be like. It's not going to be easy."

"If you break things off with me I can assure you that I will go to the police with everything that I know. How do you think life on the run is going to be then?"

"You shouldn't threaten me." His voice grew deeper. Samantha's heart raced. Was she about to witness an attack? Would the man do something to silence his female companion? If he did, would she be able to stop him?

"It's not a threat, it's a promise. You pulled me into all of this, and I did whatever I could for you. Now, you owe me. I'm not going to suffer through a broken heart while you get to go off and do whatever you please. This is real to me, isn't it real to you?"

"It is. You know it is. But that's not what this is about right now. We have to keep our heads clear, and make the right choices. One mistake is going to change everything."

"Just be patient. No one is going to care much longer. All of this will go away," the woman said.

"I'm not sure that I can do that. I feel like a sitting duck."

"That's what they want. The police will pressure you until you crack. Just keep focused on the fact that no one really cared about May. No one is going to fight for her murder to be solved. She's gone, and soon people will forget that she ever even existed."

Silence from both of them followed her words. Samantha bit into her bottom lip to prevent herself from saying anything. She wanted to shout at them both that it wasn't true. May mattered to her, and her friends, and they were going to find out the truth. But with the tension de-escalating, she knew it was best to remain silent.

"We can't meet like this again. It's too risky,"

the man said.

"You haven't even called or texted me. I have no idea what is going on with you."

"You don't need to know. I will tell you when you need to know something," the man said.

"I mean it, if you disappear, I'm going to make sure you pay."

"Stop threatening me!" He barked his words so suddenly that a small gasp escaped Samantha. She covered her mouth with her palm and closed her eyes. Had they heard her? Would they know that they were being watched? When she opened her eyes again, the figures were gone. She heard the door lock. Her heart raced. Had they left that fast? She cringed as she realized that she'd missed her opportunity to find out who they were.

Cautiously, Samantha stood up and crept to the door. With each step she expected one of them to leap out at her. Instead, she made it to the door and turned the lock and opened it just in time to see a pair of tail lights disappear. Whoever was there, at least one of them had driven. How could she have been so stupid? She never should have closed her eyes. She stepped outside and closed the door behind her.

"Samantha!"

She jumped so high that she thought she might have set a new record.

"Eddy! Don't do that!" She glared at him.

"I'm sorry, I thought you saw me, what's wrong?"

Samantha shook her head and closed her eyes. He reached out and curled his hands over her shoulders. The warmth of his touch offered her some comfort, but she didn't want to tell him what happened. She didn't want him to know how close she'd been to solving the case, and that she'd let the killer slip away.

"Why are you here, Eddy?"

"I had another hunch. You weren't at your villa, so I figured I'd take a look around the outside of the community center to see if anything might have been overlooked. I didn't expect to find you here. Were you in there alone?"

"Yes. Well, no." She frowned.

"What's wrong, Samantha? Did someone hurt you?" His eyes glowed despite the dark that surrounded them. She could see the hardness in his expression, as if he intended to protect her from anything and everything.

"No, no one hurt me. I'm just very, very, foolish."

"I know that's not true. What happened?"

Samantha heard a snap of a twig. She jumped again. Eddy wrapped his arm around her as he looked around in the direction of the twig.

"Not here. We need to find some place to talk." She shivered at the thought that either person could be watching her. If the killer and his accomplice knew that she heard their conversation, she might be next on the list.

"Okay, let's go back to your villa." He kept his arm around her as he steered her across the street to the sidewalk that wound its way down through the villas. The more she thought about it, the more she realized that she needed to tell Eddy everything. When they got inside her villa she gestured to the couch.

"Take a seat."

He sat down on the couch and looked up at her. "What is it?"

"Before I tell you this, I want you to promise that you will remain calm."

"Calm? I'm already stressed. Just tell me what it is."

"I might have overheard something while I was in the community center."

"Overheard who?"

"I'm not sure. I couldn't tell who it was, because my ears are still ringing from the explosion. But I did hear a lot of what they said."

"They?"

"A man, and a woman."

"A couple?"

"That's what it sounded like, yes. I can't be sure, but I think they were discussing May's murder."

"Why didn't you tell me right away?"

"Because I let them get away. I didn't even get a good look at them. When I should have been waiting for the chance, I closed my eyes. What is wrong with me?"

"What is wrong with you? Nothing is wrong with you. We witnessed an explosion, a woman you considered a friend is dead, of course you're a little shaken-up."

"Still, if I had only paid attention, this murder could be solved right now."

"Do you think it's possible that it was Reynold and Valerie?"

"I can't say that it wasn't, but I can't confidently say that it was. For all I know it could have been Daniel and Valerie, or Daniel and someone else. Or anyone, really." She shook her

213

head.

"If you think about it, you might be able to figure it out. Just try to rest tonight and in the morning we'll meet up in the community center. Everything might become clearer then."

"All right." She yawned and shook her head. "I guess I could try to go back to sleep." She shivered a little.

"Do you want me to stay, Samantha?" His eyes locked with hers. Samantha's heart skipped a beat as she realized that she did. Never before had she felt the need to have someone else with her, but after the explosion and the conversation she overheard she felt like company.

"Well, you're already here. You could stay if you want."

He smiled a little. "That's not exactly what I asked. I'll stay."

She stood up from the couch and grabbed him a blanket and pillow. When she returned he was already stretched out. As strange as it was to see him settled in, it was also quite comforting. When she laid down, she fell asleep easily.

Chapter Eighteen

The next morning Samantha woke up to the smell of coffee. She dressed quickly and walked into the kitchen to find Eddy. He waved to her as he squinted at her computer screen.

"I hope you don't mind. I couldn't sleep last night, so I decided to do some hunting of my own."

"On the computer?"

"I can do a thing or two with one of these. Chris has taught me a lot."

"I don't mind." She poured herself a cup of coffee. "Did you find anything?"

"I think I might have. I managed to find two old articles from a fishing magazine that had been uploaded to the internet. Can I use the printer?"

"Of course."

He picked up his own cup of coffee as the printer started up. "So, what did you find?" She sat down beside him.

"I'm not sure yet. I have a hunch, and it's a crazy one, but I just have to check it out." He stood up and retrieved the articles he had printed, and stared down at them. "It's right there in front of my face, but I still don't believe it." He stumbled back as the paper trembled in his hand.

"Eddy? You okay?" Samantha stood up and put a hand on the small of his back to steady him. "What is it?"

"Look familiar?" He held up the article and pointed to the photograph so that she could see. Her eyes widened the moment that she looked at the faces of the two young men in the picture. The article was about a Mariner fishing competition. They were smiling and one of the men had a fish on the end of his line.

"Is that Reynold?"

"It is. And his brother, Jacob."

"Jacob, who was killed?"

"Yes." Eddy shook his head. "I don't know

217

how I could have missed this. It was right under our nose."

"What do you mean? We know that Reynold was Jacob's brother and that they looked very similar."

"No, this." He pointed to a scar above the eyebrow of one of the nearly identical men in the photograph. "See the scar."

"Yes."

"And this is a photograph of Reynold taken at the trivia night last month." He held up another photograph.

"So? Reynold has a scar."

"He does!" He held up another photograph that only had one of the brothers on it. He pointed to the picture. "I never noticed it, but look at his eyebrow."

Samantha stared at the photograph. "There is a scar."

"Exactly. A scar. But look at the caption, this

is Jacob not Reynold."

"So, maybe they both had a scar?"

"In exactly the same spot? See how the hair of his eyebrow is thick everywhere, but over the scar?"

"Yes, you're right." She frowned. "So what does this mean?"

"It means that this." He pointed to the man without the scar in the first picture of the brothers. "Is not Jacob."

"But it can't be Reynold. Reynold has the scar." Her mouth grew dry. "Wait a minute." Her mind spun as she tried to fit the pieces together.

"Yes. The Reynold that we know, the Reynold that lives in Sage Gardens, has a scar."

"Does this mean what I think it means?"

"It means that it isn't Jacob that drowned in the lake at all, it was Reynold. Jacob is still very much alive, and living in our neighborhood."

Samantha's eyes widened. "Are you kidding?

How is that possible?"

"Remember how Walt turned up all of that information on Jacob's financial issues. He was involved in the scam, broke, nearly bankrupt, and didn't have much hope of a strong financial future?"

"Yes." Samantha nodded. "So you think that when Reynold drowned, Jacob decided to take his name so he could have a new life?"

"Why not? No one needed to know that it was Reynold, not Jacob that died. As far as the police were concerned it was an accident, and there was no reason to investigate further. Maybe if they had, they would have noticed the scar. Then again, maybe not."

"Maybe." Samantha began to pace back and forth. "How is this even possible? Can a man lie that well? Can he just take over his brother's life, and no one notices?"

"He likely moved away as soon as he could. With their parents already being dead and neither of them having any other family, there was no one to contest it. Jacob saw his chance and seized it."

"In a million years I never would have put that together. So Jacob and his brother Reynold go out on a boat together. Maybe they argue over Jacob's finances. Maybe Reynold didn't fall out of the boat, maybe Jacob pushed him out of anger, then saw his opportunity."

"That might be what happened. I don't know if we'll ever know for sure what happened on the boat, but I am certain that the man we know as Reynold is not Reynold at all, it's Jacob. Maybe Jacob went out there with the plan to murder his brother and steal his identity. If he did, he's certainly malicious enough to murder May. Maybe she suspected him and that's why she printed the article."

"But there were no photographs in the article."

"None that we saw. We don't know if she burned more paper in the fire. Or maybe she printed the article for another reason. I suppose she could have known about it the whole time, and even helped him to cover it up."

"No, I don't think so." Samantha stared down at the photograph of the man without the scar, the man she now knew was actually Reynold. "May wasn't the type to hide a secret like that. I think she found him out, and she wanted to give him the chance to explain himself. Remember, she mentioned something about the scar to Daniel. Maybe she would have even forgiven him, that was the type of person that May was." She sighed. "She cared."

"So now, it's very possible that we're not just dealing with one murder, but two."

"Yes, it is. But how can we prove any of it? All we have are guesses and hunches. Nothing solid. I doubt any officer will make an arrest based on a small scar."

"Maybe, but I might be able to convince the police to do a DNA test."

"I don't think that's going to work, Eddy. This was a very long time ago, there's not going to be DNA on file for Reynold. They would have to exhume his body, and they're not going to do that based on a hunch."

"Ah, you're right, I didn't really think that through. So, how else can we get some proof? Should we search through Reynold's house?"

"He's too smart for that. Plus, there's still the bomb to consider. I think we should tail him, and see where he goes. Maybe we'll figure out whether he and Valerie are in on this together."

"Good idea."

"Although, if he is smart he won't go anywhere near her," Samantha said.

"Maybe not, but if Valerie is as determined as her past implies, then she's going to demand his attention. We can find out by tailing her, or Reynold."

"I think we're better off tailing Reynold. Valerie is a social butterfly, and we might end up running around in circles for hours."

"Okay, fair enough. We'll tail Reynold, and see what he's up to. That might give us a better clue as to what he plans to do next, too."

"On a stake out together, this should be fun." She laughed. "I guess I'd better make room for more taco wrappers."

Eddy patted his stomach. "Owen said no more tacos. We'll have to go by the burger place."

"Oh good, they have those curly fries I like."

"Woman after my own heart." He winked at her.

"Wait, we're supposed to meet Jo and Walt remember?"

"Yes, but not for a while. We'll be back by then, we can fill them in then. They both looked like they needed the rest after yesterday."

"Good point. Let's catch Reynold before he leaves the house then."

Once in the car Samantha drove towards

Reynold's villa. As she approached, she noticed that Valerie's car was in the driveway of her villa. It was tempting to follow her instead, but Reynold was the one she was truly curious about. Could he really actually be Jacob? Before she could roll up to Reynold's villa, his car backed out of the driveway. She applied the brakes and gave him a few minutes head start before she began following him.

"We're in luck. If we hadn't moved fast, we would have missed him." Eddy scooted forward in his seat. "Let's hope he leads us to something good."

Thirty minutes later Samantha rolled her eyes. "I think he's leading us on a wild goose chase."

"Where is he going?" Eddy stared through the windshield.

"I don't know, but we're getting further and further out of town. Something tells me he doesn't want to be found."

"Hang back a bit. You don't want him to catch on that he's being tailed."

"I have done this before, you know."

"I know, I know. I just wish I had some idea of where he was going."

"Wait, look we're going into a campsite. Maybe he has a cabin in here."

"A cabin in the woods. It's a perfect place to hide out until the investigation goes cold."

"Or until the wrong suspect is convicted."

"Yes, that too." Eddy pointed to some brush along a group of cabins. "Pull in here so that he can't see the car."

Samantha did as he instructed. Although the car was well hidden, they still had a clear view of the cabin where Reynold parked. He opened the car door, glanced around, then closed it and headed into the cabin. Samantha sighed as she realized that they might have hit a dead end.

"What do you think, Eddy?"

"It's a bit odd. It sure doesn't look like he's waiting for anyone."

"Maybe he's preparing to disappear."

"Maybe." Eddy narrowed his eyes.

"Well, I guess this might be a bust. Are we going to sit out here forever?"

"I didn't think that you would mind the company." He shifted in his seat and looked over at her.

Samantha blushed and looked down at her hands. "I don't."

"No?" He reached out and turned the radio on at a quiet level. "We haven't had much of a chance to talk about life lately."

"We've been too busy living it, that's a good sign."

"Sure it is, but I enjoy hearing your opinion on things."

"That's going to have to wait. Because here comes Valerie." She pointed through the side window and ducked down nearly on to Eddy's chest as the woman slid out of the backseat of Reynold's car. "I don't think he knew she was there."

"Mmhm, and where does she think she's going?" Eddy leaned forward as Samantha straightened up. While they watched Valerie walked right up the dirt driveway to the cabin.

"She's a fool if she thinks that Reynold is going to care for her the way that she wants." Eddy frowned.

"Maybe she's not as involved as we thought. Maybe she's just lovesick."

Valerie paused in front of the door. She looked around for a moment, then raised her hand and knocked. A second later the door swung open and Valerie disappeared.

"We're going to have to get closer if we want to hear what she's saying."

"Samantha, we need to be careful. You stay here, I'll go."

"I don't think so." She pushed her door open and stepped out. She was already halfway through the side yard when she realized Eddy was right behind her. They both paused beside some bushes near the living room window. Although it was closed, it was not snapped tight, so the voices drifted through the small space.

"Why would you come here? How many times do I have to tell you this?"

"Relax. No one has anything on you. I think you're right we should disappear. Let's leave tonight. I don't want to wait around any longer. Let's just go."

"I told you, you're not invited."

"Don't do this to me, Reynold. I'm the only one who understands you. I know why you did what you did. I forgive you for it. We can start a new life together."

"You forgive me for it?" He laughed. "For which part?"

"You had no choice. May found out about

your past, she figured it out, and you were going to end up in prison. It's not like you wanted her to die, but you had no choice."

"You're right about that. The last thing I wanted to do was kill her. But that nosy fool couldn't just leave things alone. But, that doesn't change anything, Valerie, life on the run is no place for a woman like you."

"Let me decide that. Look what I did for you. I know, it didn't exactly work out. But I did try. If only it was Daniel that opened that door instead of Samantha and her little crew. He would have been gone, too."

"I never asked you to do that. It's made things worse for me now. Before Daniel was the main suspect in May's death. Now everyone is focused on me. Don't you see how that caused me more problems?"

"Yes. But he was a threat to you. I couldn't resist. I needed to protect you. That's how much I love you."

"Oh Valerie. I wish this was a different time, a different life, you're such a good woman."

"It can be different. Don't you see? All you have to do is let it. Please, Reynold, let me be part of your life. I have nothing if I don't have you."

"Valerie, you're asking for too much. I don't have time for this now. Maybe if things blow over I can come back for you. Then we can figure some things out together. But for now, I have to handle this myself."

"I can't believe that you would betray me like this."

"I am trying to protect you."

"You're a liar. You just used me, didn't you? You were never going to marry me or take me away from here. You just wanted a way to get close to May and you figured it would be through me. How awful."

"That's not true. I love you, too, Valerie. But my life doesn't allow for that. I've practically been on the run since I was in my twenties, and honestly I don't know how not to be."

"I can teach you. If you let me."

Eddy looked over at Samantha and rolled his eyes. In that moment neither of them noticed the front door swing open. It wasn't until Samantha felt something pressed against the back of her neck that she realized their mistake.

Chapter Nineteen

"Eddy." Samantha didn't dare to take another breath. When he looked over at her his eyes widened.

"Don't move, Samantha."

"Actually, do move, Samantha." Samantha's heart raced as she heard Reynold's voice. "You too, Eddy. Both of you on your feet. If you make one false move you're both dead."

Cautiously, Samantha slowly stood up. Eddy followed suit, with his eyes locked to hers.

"Just be calm, Samantha. Do whatever he says."

"That's right, Samantha. March." Reynold pointed with the gun towards his car. Samantha crept forward keeping her steps as small as possible. She wanted to delay getting into the car as long as possible.

"We'll do anything you ask, Reynold. Just

don't hurt us," Samantha said.

"It's a little late for that. Valerie, open the trunk."

"Reynold, think about this," Valerie said.

"I am."

"Why not just kill them here? No one will find them."

Samantha stared at Valerie with disbelief. Even though she already knew Valerie was a potential killer, it was hard for her to believe that she would encourage him to kill them both.

"Not here. Get in." He pointed to the trunk.

The gaping mouth of the trunk stared up at Samantha. She felt Eddy's hand slip into hers.

"I'll get in first."

"Fine, I don't care," Reynold said.

Samantha watched as Eddy climbed into the trunk. She knew it hurt him to do so, but he didn't make a sound. Her heart sunk as she realized that it might be the last place they were both alive. She thought about screaming, but with the distance they were into the woods she knew that no one would hear. She climbed into the trunk after Eddy. It was a tight squeeze. The moment the trunk closed, he wrapped his arm around her.

"It's going to be okay, Samantha."

"I don't think it is, Eddy."

"It is." He gave her a gentle squeeze. "Just try to stay calm. We've found our way out of tight spots before."

Samantha closed her eyes as the engine started. Wherever Reynold intended to take them, she was sure it was their final destination. Eddy held on to her for the entire drive. She heard him mumbling, but couldn't make out what he was saying. Though Eddy didn't strike her as a religious person, she guessed that he might be praying. When the car lurched to a stop, Eddy pressed his lips close to her ear.

"I counted the distance. It's about the same distance that we drove from Sage Gardens."

"You counted every second?"

"It's the best way to figure out where we are. We could be back in town."

"Or we could be even further away," Samantha said.

"You're right."

The trunk popped open and sunlight blinded Samantha. Reynold leaned over the trunk.

"Get out and stay low. If anyone sees you, they're dead, too."

Samantha climbed out of the trunk and recognized the back of the community center. A scream welled up in her throat, but she knew that Reynold would make good on his threat if she cried out. Did she want to risk being responsible for anyone else dying?

Samantha discreetly fumbled in her pocket for her cell phone. She couldn't see it to place a call, so she just pressed one of the buttons she knew by feel. She often used the recorder on her phone when researching stories she wanted to look into, or instructions that she was worried she wouldn't remember. Even if they were killed, she could leave evidence behind for the detectives. Eddy climbed out of the trunk behind her. He kept his head down as well. Reynold herded them to the back door of the community center.

"Unlock it."

"It should be open." Samantha gulped out.

"No, it isn't. I requested that it remain closed because of the memorial service for May later this afternoon. We'll have the place to ourselves. I did good, right Reynold?" Valerie kissed his cheek. Samantha tried not to grimace. Valerie unlocked the door and Reynold shoved them both inside.

"Against the table." Reynold directed Eddy towards the long snack table near the back of the room. Eddy and Samantha began to move towards the table.

"No, not you, Samantha. You get over here. Right here." Reynold pointed to the spot beside him, with the gun pointed at Samantha.

Samantha's feet froze to the ground.

"Don't move, Samantha." Eddy looked over at her. "Just stay calm."

"Hey, if she doesn't move, then Val goes, and then the two of you go next. I'll let you pick who goes first. So what's it going to be, Samantha?"

Samantha's stomach churned as she recalled the way she tried to comfort Reynold after May's death. The whole time he was the killer. She was very disappointed in her instincts.

"I'm not going to move."

"You are." He released the safety. "Three, two..."

"Samantha don't..."

"I'm here." Samantha stopped right beside Reynold. "I'm here, don't hurt anyone. Reynold, don't you think that you've done enough damage here? Are you really going to kill three more people?"

"Does it matter now?" He shook his head. "It

seems to be the only thing I'm good at. I started off with my brother."

"You killed your own brother?" Eddy stared at him. "Why would you do a thing like that?"

"Because he had everything. I got wrapped up in Daniel's little scam. It was supposed to make me a millionaire. Instead it left me penniless. But John, the know it all, who warned me not to get involved with any of it, was still flush with cash. He had everyone's respect. He had the good life. I was bankrupt, being investigated for fraud, and on my way to a terrible life. One night, we went out on the fishing boat together. We argued about the decisions I'd made, and even though I didn't plan on it, I just got so mad, I shoved him over the side of the boat. It just happened."

"Okay, yes, it happened, but what matters is what you're going to do now." Eddy tried to meet his eyes. Samantha stared at Eddy as she remained by Reynold's side. Eddy shook his head a little, but didn't dare to step forward. She got the message. He didn't want her to do anything risky.

"What about May?" Eddy asked. "Why did you kill her?"

"May spoke to Valerie about her suspicions. May figured it out. I never expected her to, but she did. She remembered the scar on Jacob's eyebrow, my eyebrow. I got it when I was with her, I fell off my bike. A scar that Reynold of course didn't have. That's when she began to suspect that I wasn't Reynold at all. It's been so many years since anyone called me Jacob, but when she did, I knew that I had to shut her up before she told the whole world what I did."

"What is your end game here? Do you really think you're going to get away with all of this?" Eddy asked.

"I don't care. That's what you don't seem to understand. No matter what happens, you three are a liability. Just like May was."

"What about Daniel?" Samantha looked over at him. "Isn't Daniel an issue that you need to deal with, too?"

"Daniel?" He shook his head. "Not at all. He will never do anything because if he does he has to dredge all the decisions of his past up and put himself at risk again because he turned on the other investors in the scheme. He despised May. Even if she told him something because she suspected me of murder, or being an impostor, he wouldn't have done anything. May might have told Daniel but that doesn't matter. Unfortunately, she told her suspicions to Valerie. This one, thought it would be a good idea to off him, not me." He shot a look in Valerie's direction. "She got caught up in emotion, I don't do that. That's what changed everything. Then I became the prime suspect."

"Daniel was onto you. He was going to reveal your identity," Valerie said.

"Daniel? Daniel couldn't identify his own nose. He's an idiot. You did it because you wanted to, not for me."

"That's not true Jacob..."

"Stop calling me that, just please, stop calling me that."

"All right, Reynold." Eddy stepped forward. "How about this, I know that John didn't just drown. He was a strong swimmer, and he wasn't a drinker, was he? When you shoved him out of that boat, he didn't just disappear, did he?"

"That's all in the past." He hung his head for a moment. "That day, that day changed my life. I never thought I'd make anything of myself, but then I did. I just did. John kept on and on about how stupid I was to fall for Daniel's scheme, and then he stood up. He kept blathering on about how I ruined my life and how I would never be anything but a fool. And all I could think was, I'm not the fool that's standing up in a boat, am I? Then it happened, I shoved him, right into the water. I thought, that was going to be it. He'd get back in the boat, and have even more reason to dislike me. Then I saw his hands grab the side of the boat. I thought, grab your brother's hand, he needs your help. But when I touched his hand, I thought about what it would be like to never hear his voice again. I shoved his hands off the boat. He called for help, but every time he grabbed for the boat, I just shoved his hands away. I never really thought about it, I just kept shoving. At some point, he stopped grabbing. It didn't dawn on me until several minutes passed, that I'd done it. I'd gone from being a failure to being a success. That was how it began."

"Your brother never gave you a chance to prove yourself. Now you have that, now you can decide to be a better man and put down that gun. Maybe he was wrong. Maybe you just made a mistake and needed a chance to recover from it. Now, you can start telling the truth."

"Oh no, Eddy, you don't understand. That was only how it began, my chance to become the man I should have been. And now this is how it ends." He raised the gun again and pointed it in Eddy's direction.

"No, don't!" Samantha pleaded as she stepped towards Reynold.

243

"Samantha, stop!" Eddy's heart dropped the moment he saw her move. He started to move towards her to shield her, but Reynold swung the gun towards her before he could take a step.

"Not a step, Eddy, or she'll be first." He kept the gun pointed at her. "I don't have anything to lose, remember? One by one, I'll eliminate any threat to my freedom."

"Please, this isn't really you. Think about it. We can let them go. Samantha hasn't done anything to you. This isn't what you want. We're in love!" Valerie grasped at the hand that held the gun. Samantha was surprised at Valerie's sudden change of heart, she seemed ready for Reynold to get rid of them a few minutes ago.

"Back off!" He swung his hand back and knocked her to the ground. "I'm not in love, you dimwit. Jacob drowned in that lake. Maybe it was my brother, John, who actually died, but so did the man that I once was. The one that had no future, the one that fell for some lying fool's con. All I wanted was another chance at life, an opportunity to be the person I was meant to be before May's brother came along and ruined everything. I could have had an amazing life. I could have done everything right. I wasn't stupid, I was just young, and Daniel was a charmer. He preyed on me because he knew I was jealous of John's success, just like he was jealous of his sister." He glared as he lifted the gun back towards Eddy. "All I wanted was a chance to start over. So John had to die, and I got that chance. Then I started using his middle name, Reynold, and I had the clean slate that I wanted, that I needed. But someone eventually had to find out, and unfortunately that was May, and she had to die, and now it's you, Eddy, along with Samantha, and Valerie of course. But you first." He pointed the gun at Eddy.

"Eddy!" Samantha started to lunge forward, but she knew she was too far away to get to Reynold in time. Her heart raced as she waited for the sound of the gunshot.

Chapter Twenty

Before Reynold could pull the trigger, there was a loud bang at the front door. It made everyone in the room jump. As all of their attention turned to the door, a figure surged towards Reynold from behind him. He sprang up into the air and tackled the man, with one arm around the hand that held the gun. The weapon discharged and a bullet whizzed through the air. Samantha turned back to see Walt on the floor. He wrestled with Reynold for the gun. Samantha grabbed the only thing that was nearby, a brand new fire poker. She swung it down hard against the back of Reynold's head. He jolted, then collapsed. Walt wrenched the gun from his grasp and looked up at Samantha.

"Are you okay?"

"I think so. Are you?"

"Yes." Walt nodded. He looked down at the man on the floor.

"I didn't kill him did I?" Samantha's eyes widened in horror. Walt crouched down beside him and felt for a pulse on the side of his neck.

"No, you didn't kill him. He's just knocked out. He'll have quite a headache though."

Samantha felt some relief as she turned towards Eddy. "Are you okay?"

Eddy looked past her, at the door. "She's getting away!"

Valerie ran for the door. When she pushed it open, Jo greeted her with her arm outstretched. Valerie ran right into it and fell backwards onto the floor.

"Stay down, or you won't have such a pretty face anymore." Jo glared down at her.

"Why? What did I do?" She gulped as she stared up at Jo. "I'm a victim here. He conned me, just like he conned everybody else!"

"I don't think so." Eddy walked over to her to keep an eye on her. "You're the one that built the bomb and put it on Daniel's car. That's attempted

247

murder. You're on the hook, just like your boyfriend over there. So, at least you'll spend the rest of your years in the same place, just on opposite sides of the building."

"No, no, you can't do this to me. Eddy! Samantha! You know me! I'm just like you!"

"Quiet. You're nothing like me." Samantha folded her arms across her chest. "Not after what the two of you did to May, not after what you almost did to Daniel, and to Jo. You're going to pay for it."

"You'll never be able to prove anything."

"I don't need to prove it, I recorded it." Samantha pulled out her cell phone and pressed play on the recording. The entire conversation began to play back. "Do you think you're going to flirt your way out of that, Valerie?"

"Samantha, please."

"No, any chance of sympathy from me ended the moment you almost blew up my friend. You are just as responsible for May's death. You told

Reynold about her suspicions. You knew how dangerous the situation was and instead of warning her, you stood by and let it happen. If it were up to me, you'd also be knocked out on the floor." She glared into Valerie's eyes. "In fact, I can still arrange that if you want to try to run again."

"No, no, I won't." She covered her head just as sirens blared from outside.

"Oh no." Jo glanced over her shoulder through the door. "The police are here. I should take off."

"No." Eddy remained by Reynold, who was still knocked out cold on the floor. "Don't leave."

"What? Why not?" She frowned.

"You haven't done anything wrong, Jo. You don't have anything to hide. You shouldn't have to run."

Jo looked between Walt, Eddy, and Samantha. "What if they think I had something to do with it?"

"They won't." Walt stepped closer to her.

"I don't want to end up in handcuffs." Jo crossed her arms.

"They'll have to go through me first." Samantha put her hands on her hips.

"And me." Walt stepped up beside Samantha.

"And me." Eddy tipped his hat. "Trust me, they don't want to try to put handcuffs on me."

"I don't know."

"It's too late now." Walt tilted his head towards the door just before it was yanked open. Samantha dropped the fire poker to the floor and raised her hands in the air. Her friends followed suit. Within a few minutes Valerie and Reynold were handcuffed. Reynold was barely awake as he was hauled into a police car.

"What happened?"

"You got caught, that's what." Eddy stared into his eyes. "Now, finally there is justice, not just for May, but for John as well. You will never be him again, you never were, this whole time you've been, Jacob, the same person that you always were."

He growled and tried to lunge towards Eddy, but the police officer forced him into the back of the police car.

"Try not to get him too riled up, Eddy," the officer said.

"Sorry." Eddy cleared his throat. He turned back towards the community center to see Walt, Samantha, and Jo all knotted together. Despite the tension of the circumstances he couldn't help but smile. There were three people he could count on, no matter what happened. It might have been the first time he'd ever had that many people in his life that he could trust. As he walked back over to them Jo smiled at him.

"Thanks Eddy."

"For what?"

"For showing me that I'm not a criminal."

"You're not. You're a private eye now,

remember?" He winked at her.

"I'm not so sure about that. Maybe I'm not cut out for going solo."

"You'll never have to worry about that." Samantha wrapped her arm around her shoulders. "Whether you like it or not." Samantha chuckled.

"She's right." Walt nodded.

"How did you two know where we were?" Eddy looked between them.

"To be honest, we didn't." Jo shook her head. "When you two didn't show up when we agreed to meet we decided to check things out for ourselves, and that's when we stumbled across the situation. You really should have told us what you were up to."

"Yes." Walt fixed them both with a stern stare. "You should have clued us in."

"We got caught up in the moment, literally. We were listening in one moment, then at gunpoint the next. We had no idea where they were taking us."

"I still have no idea why they brought us back here." Eddy pulled off his hat and scratched the top of his head.

"I think I know why." Walt smiled. "He was going to use Valerie to take the fall. He would have shot you all, but made it look like it was Valerie who did it and then killed herself. Classic frame job. He would have been long gone before the detectives figured out that Valerie wasn't the shooter. After all, it wouldn't take them long to put together that she had a key to the community center and she was the one who planted the bomb, then they would have no reason to suspect him. Pretty smart if you ask me."

"Walt." Jo knocked his ankle with the tip of her boot.

"What?" Walt frowned. "It was quite clever."

"That's our friends you're talking about him murdering, you know?"

"But they're fine, right?" He smiled at

Samantha and Eddy.

"Thanks to the two of you." Eddy pulled his hat back on his head. "Jo's right, no more flying solo for any of us."

"Agreed." Samantha nodded.

"I'm going to head to the police station. I want to fill Chris in on what happened."

"I of course, need to shower." Walt brushed off the sleeves of his dress shirt. "I have to say tackling is a bit more fun than I expected, but the filth that comes with it is intolerable." He shuddered.

"Don't worry, Walt, it washes off." Jo brushed a bit of dust from the collar of his shirt.

"I hope so. I will probably have to burn this shirt though." He muttered as he walked away. Samantha laughed as she watched him go.

"Just when I think he's loosened up a little bit."

"Maybe Walt is just fine the way he is." Jo

tilted her head to the side. "I used to think his quirks were more than a little irritating, but the more I get to know him the more I understand his rituals. Maybe they don't make sense to us, but they sure do to him."

"Hey, that's all that matters, right?" Samantha patted her back. "Thanks for being there, Jo. I thought we were done for."

"Don't worry, Samantha, like you told me before, I've always got your back." She waved to her as she headed off towards her villa. Samantha started to walk towards hers, when she caught sight of a familiar face near May's memorial. Without a second thought she walked over to Owen and placed her hand on his shoulder.

"It's over now, Owen."

"Is it?" He looked over at her. "I just keep thinking, if I had arrived just a little earlier, maybe I could have stopped all of this."

"Owen, there was no chance. May's death would have happened anyway. If you had interrupted it, it just would have happened at another time."

"What do you mean?"

"I mean Reynold knew he was going to kill her from the moment he knew she was a threat to his new life. When she found that article, he already knew he was going to kill her. She wanted to give him the chance to explain, and when he knew what she'd figured out he had no choice but to kill her."

"At least you didn't let her murderer get away with it," Owen said.

Samantha stared at the collection of flowers and knew in that moment that there was one more thing she wasn't going to let someone get away with. As she walked back to her villa she dialed Daniel's number.

"What do you want?"

"Have you heard from the police?"

"Yes, I have. So now you know, I didn't murder my sister."

256

"Maybe you didn't do the crime, Daniel, but I think it's time you treat her with some kindness."

"Why should I do that?"

"Because you're her brother and it's time for you to be her family. You're the only one who can be."

The silence on the other end of the phone made Samantha doubt that Daniel even listened to what she had to say. However, after a few seconds passed he cleared his throat.

"All right, I'll give her a proper funeral. I suppose, I can do that."

"Thank you, Daniel. If you need any help, I am at your disposal."

"You never really felt a connection with me, Samantha, did you?"

"I'm sorry, Daniel, no I didn't."

"That's all right, I didn't either, it was just another con. One of these days I'm going to have to find a way to be honest. Maybe that will be part of my new life."

"Maybe it will." Samantha hung up the phone and opened the door to her villa. As much as she grieved for May's loss, and in some ways grieved for a man, John Reynold Smith, that she'd never even met, she was relieved that the crime was solved, and May would have the send-off that she deserved.

The End

More Cozy Mysteries by Cindy Bell

Sage Gardens Cozy Mysteries

Birthdays Can Be Deadly

Money Can Be Deadly

Trust Can Be Deadly

Ties Can Be Deadly

Rocks Can Be Deadly

Numbers Can Be Deadly

Chocolate Centered Cozy Mysteries

The Sweet Smell of Murder

A Deadly Delicious Delivery

A Treacherous Tasty Trail

Luscious Pastry at a Lethal Party

Dune House Cozy Mysteries

Seaside Secrets

Boats and Bad Guys

Treasured History

Hidden Hideaways

Dodgy Dealings

Suspects and Surprises

Heavenly Highland Inn Cozy Mysteries

Murdering the Roses

Dead in the Daisies

Killing the Carnations

Drowning the Daffodils

Suffocating the Sunflowers

Books, Bullets and Blooms

A Deadly serious Gardening Contest

A Bridal Bouquet and a Body

Wendy the Wedding Planner Cozy Mysteries

Matrimony, Money and Murder

Chefs, Ceremonies and Crimes

Knives and Nuptials

Mice, Marriage and Murder

Bekki the Beautician Cozy Mysteries

Hairspray and Homicide

A Dyed Blonde and a Dead Body

Mascara and Murder

Pageant and Poison

Conditioner and a Corpse

Mistletoe, Makeup and Murder

Hairpin, Hair Dryer and Homicide

Blush, a Bride and a Body

Shampoo and a Stiff

Cosmetics, a Cruise and a Killer

Lipstick, a Long Iron and Lifeless

Camping, Concealer and Criminals

Treated and Dyed

Printed in Great Britain
by Amazon